THE GUNSMITH

430

The Show Girl

THE GUNSMITH

430

The Show Girl

J.R. Roberts

SPEAKING VOLUMES, LLC
NAPLES, FLORIDA
2017

The Show Girl

ISBN 978-1-62815-748-2

Chapter One

Denver, Colorado

Part of going to Denver, for Clint Adams, was seeing his good friend, Talbot Roper, who was also the best private detective in the country. Naturally, there were some times when he came to town that Roper was away on business. This time, however, the detective was not on the road, and was eager to visit with Clint.

There was no girl in Roper's outer office, which was not unusual. He didn't employ anyone on a regular basis, and there was a secretarial school just down the block where he often plucked someone to employ.

Roper was sitting back in his chair, feet on his desk and hands clasped behind his head when Clint walked in.

"What the hell—" Roper said, dropping his feet to the floor. "Why didn't you send me a telegram you were coming?"

"Because I didn't know until yesterday," Clint said. "Besides, how often do I get a chance to catch you at your desk, lounging."

Roper came around the desk and gave Clint a warm handshake. They had been friends a long time, had a lot in common—not the least of which was working with Allan Pinkerton during the Civil War. Roper had often asked Clint to come in as a partner, because he had natural ability as a detective. They had worked together on cases many times, but Clint always turned down that offer—just as he had turned down Pinkerton's offers to be one of his agents. He just didn't like the idea of working for anyone, or even with anyone, on a permanent basis.

"Sit down," Roper said. "Let me get you a drink. A short whiskey before I take you out to lunch."

"Okay," Clint said, "A short one."

"Where are you staying?" Roper asked. "The usual place?"

The "usual place" when he was in Denver was the Denver House Hotel.

"Yep." He accepted the glass of whiskey.

Roper took his glass back behind his desk.

"They should be giving you a discount there, after all your stays," he said.

"Hey, I'll mention that as I check out. What's got you relaxing at your desk?"

"I don't have a case."

"That's unusual, isn't it?"

"Very," Roper said. "I don't know what to do with myself. It's great to see you."

"I'm glad to find you here, Tal," Clint said. "I was afraid you'd be away. Now we can catch up."

Roper smiled. "Hey, there's a new dance hall. We should check it out together, tonight."

"Sure," Clint said. "I've got nothing to do. I'm here to see you."

"I'm flattered," Roper said. "How many times do we meet when neither one of us needs back-up from the other?"

"You're right," Clint said, raising his glass. "To nobody trying to kill us."

"I'll drink to that!"

***

They drank to it, then drank again before going out to have lunch at one of Roper's nearby haunts.

It was a small place, with not much of a storefront to attract people.

"It's all locals," Roper told Clint, as they sat at his regular back table.

"Mr. Roper!" A man came running over. "How nice to have you back."

"Hello, Pete. This is my friend, Clint Adams. Clint, this is Pete Reynolds. He owns this place."

Reynolds executed a small bow with his hands clasped together and said, "Any friend of Mr. Roper's is welcome here."

"Thank you."

"The usual, sir?" he asked Roper.

"The beef stew is their specialty," Roper told Clint.

"Sounds good."

"Two beef stews, Pete."

"I'll have Alex bring it over right away," the man said.

Reynolds looked to Clint to be in his mid-40's, with a head of curly black hair that was shot with gray, and a mustache to match.

"Pete opened this place a couple of years ago, had some trouble with a few locals who wanted a piece of the action. I helped him out."

"Does he make you pay when you come in?"

"I insist."

"Good," Clint said, "I was going to insist, too."

"Okay," Roper said, "now tell me what's been going on, and then I'll do the same."

"Well," Clint said, "I was just in Washington D.C. . . ."

Chapter Two

Clint and Roper went their separate ways after lunch. Roper promised to come and get him at his hotel later that evening, so they could go to the new dance hall.

"I suppose you helped the owner of that place out of a jam, too, huh?"

"Don't even know him," Roper said. "We're gonna see the place for the first time together."

"I'll look forward to it. Meanwhile, I'll need a new suit of clothes for the occasion."

"I can loan you one."

"Thanks, but I prefer my own."

"I can take you to the store where I buy my clothes."

"Thanks again, but I feel like a walk, and I'm sure I'll find a store along the way."

"There are a lot of them," Roper said. "Have yourself a shopping spree."

"Not what I had in mind," Clint said, "but I'll have a look around. . ."

They agreed to meet at the hotel, and went their separate ways.

***

Clint found a small store specializing in men's clothing, and spent some time there with a willing and eager clerk. He left with not one, but two new suits of clothes, as well as a couple of new shirts he could wear during the day.

He went back to his hotel and arranged for a hot bath, then took it in a long and languid manner, his gun nearby on a chair. He'd had too many baths interrupted in the past by somebody trying to kill him.

After the bath he went to his room and tried on the new suits. Satisfied with one, he set it aside to wear when the time came.

He was still working his way through a Jules Verne book, so he sat and read a couple of chapters before checking the time. When he had a half an hour left before meeting Roper he set the book aside, and slipped into his new clothes. He felt like a different man, but he had to buckle his gunbelt around his waist, which made him feel more like himself.

He left the room and went down to the Denver House's bar. He was slowly working his way through a beer when Talbot Roper arrived.

"How about a beer before we go?" Clint asked, as the detective approached him.

"I'd never say no to that," Roper said.

Clint ordered a fresh beer for Roper, while he continued to work on his.

"You look splendid," Roper said. "That's a heckuva suit."

Clint looked at Roper's own suit and tie and said, "This style fits you a lot better than it fits me."

"Well," Roper said, shrugging his shoulders, "I do have to have mine tailored to accommodate this." He touched the gun in the holster beneath his left arm,

"It hardly shows," Clint said.

Roper leaned in and sniffed.

"And you smell soapy," he said. "That'll please the ladies we're going to meet tonight."

"Did you make arrangements for that?'

"No," He said, "I just know what the night life is like in Denver, don't you? Two handsome specimens like us, the girls will be flocking."

"I don't know about you, my friend, but I'm getting a little too old to be called a handsome young specimen."

"I didn't say 'young,'" Roper pointed out. "Did I say 'young?'"

"No," Clint answered, "as a matter of fact, you didn't."

"Come on, drink up," Roper told him. "The night awaits."

They finished their beers and went out front to have the doorman get them a cab.

***

The place was called Molly Muldoon's Dance Hall and Emporium. From outside they could hear lively music playing inside.

"What makes it an Emporium?" Clint asked, as they approached the front door.

"I don't know," Roper said. "I guess we'll find out when we get inside."

"And do we know who Molly Muldoon is?"

"Not a clue," Roper said.

"You mean you haven't looked into this place, yet?"

"No," Roper said. "I told you, we're going to find out about it together."

The front entrance had the customary batwing doors, but as soon as they entered they could see that this was not a normal saloon. For one thing, off to the right was some kind of store, selling who knew what? They could see some garments, some knick-knacks, things you didn't usually see in a saloon.

"I guess that's what makes it an Emporium," Clint said, indicating the store.

"Well then," Roper said, "what do you say we go further inside and see what makes it a saloon and dance hall?"

"After you, Mr. Roper," Clint said, with an exaggerated bow.

Chapter Three

They entered the saloon and dance hall portion of Molly Muldoon's. It was jumping, with a full band on a stage supplying the lively music, along with some dancing girls. Off to the left was an impossibly long bar, which seemed to have little or no room at it. Likewise, all the tables in the place—and there were a lot of them—seemed to be full.

"Let's try the bar," Roper suggested.

"Lead the way," Clint said, "I'm with you."

They went to the bar where they combined their shoulders and managed to carve out space for themselves. They got a couple of hard looks, which faded when they saw something in Clint and Roper's eyes.

They waved down one of the two bartenders patrolling behind the bar and said, "Two beers."

"Comin' up!"

An obviously experienced barkeep drew two beers and slid them down to the men. Along the way customers withdrew their arms and hands to get out of the way.

Roper caught the two beers, handed Clint one and clinked glasses with him.

"Good to see you, old friend."

"Same here," Clint said.

They turned their backs to the bar and looked the interior over.

"Quite a place," Roper said.

"It sure is, but I don't see any gambling going on."

"You're right," Roper said. "Maybe it happens in another room."

"Well," Clint said, "looks like there are plenty of girls, both on the floor and on stage."

The girls working the floor were wearing brightly colored dresses and showing lots of skin. The girls on stage were also brightly attired, but not showing as much skin, as it was likely to fall out of the costumes while they danced.

"Get ready for the show, gents," one of the bartender started yelling, "get ready for the show!"

"What kind of show?" Roper asked, as the man walked past. It was the same bartender who had served them.

"Girls, Mister," he said, "dancing girls."

"Speaking of girls," Clint said, "where's Molly Muldoon?"

The bartender laughed.

"Molly's a fifty-year-old man with a pot belly and a full beard. And the money to open a place like this, but who'd come if he called it Beefy Bill's?"

"Guess you are right," Roper said, looking at Clint. "You want to get a seat somewhere?"

"I can see just fine from here," Clint said. He could also see the entire room, and the front door. Roper understood the need for that.

"Yeah, me, too."

The stage was now empty except for the band off to one side. Then a man came out and stood right in the center, wearing a tuxedo.

"Ladies and gentlemen," he called out, "The Molly Muldoon Merry Maids!"

He ran off the stage and from the other side a line of 8 girls came filing out. The band began to play and the girls started dancing. Clint noticed immediately that one girl seemed terribly out of step. She was the last one on the right, and didn't seem to belong there, at all. She was pretty enough, a slender, fair-haired girl in a blue dress. Also, she didn't seem to be quite as willing as the other girls to lift her skirts high and show her legs and bloomers.

"See that gal on the right?" Roper said.

"I know," Clint said, "how did she get up there in the first place? She should be serving drinks."

"She'd probably drop the trays."

"I feel sorry for her," Clint said. "She's probably going to get fired by Molly."

"Or Beefy Bill."

They both laughed, keeping it low.

They continued to watch as the girls danced, with the poor lass on the end struggling to keep up, and then they filed off the stage as the music came to an end.

"That was brutal," Roper said.

"You didn't like the show?" the bartender asked from behind them.

They both turned and looked at him, wondering if he was actually Beefy Bill—or Molly.

"Seven of the girls were real good," Roper said.

"It was just that one on the right," Clint added. "How did she get up there?"

"You gotta ask Lou that," the bartender said. "She hires the dancers."

"Lou is a girl?" Clint asked. "And Molly's a man?"

"That's right."

"This is a real interesting place," Clint said.

"You got that right, too, Mister," the barkeep said. "Two more?"

Chapter Four

Clint and Roper nursed their second beers and walked around, checking the place out. The band continued to play, although not the rollicking number it had produced for the dancing girls. They discovered they were right about the gambling, it was in another room entirely—poker, faro, blackjack, roulette and a huge wheel of fortune. But they weren't there to gamble, so they left that room and went back into the dance hall.

As they left the gambling room they walked past the stage and heard loud voices from behind a curtain.

". . . come on, Lou," a girl's voice said. "I'll do better next time."

"I can't afford the chance, Nell," another female voice said. Rather than a girl, this one sounded like a woman. "Once was enough."

"What do the other girls say?"

"They don't want you on stage with them," the woman said.

"Really?"

"Nellie," the woman said, "you were terrible."

"I'm just inexperienced!"

"You've been practicing with the girls for weeks, Nell," Lou argued.

Roper nudged Clint, and they kept moving.

"That poor kid," the detective said.

"Well, the other woman was right," Clint said, "She was terrible."

"You know what else is terrible?" Roper asked.

"What?"

"These beer mugs are empty."

They went back to the bar and waved the mugs at the bartender. He brought over two fresh ones.

"We gotta have something to eat after this," Roper said. "Where do you want to go?"

"You pick," Clint said, "but make it a steakhouse, will you?"

"Steakhouse it is," Roper said.

Clint sipped his beer. "I still feel bad for that girl. Why don't they just give her a job out front?"

"Maybe she doesn't want to work out front," Roper said. "Maybe she feels more comfortable on stage."

"Really?" Clint asked. "Did she look comfortable to you up there?"

Roper laughed. "You got me, there."

***

Roper chose a steakhouse that happened to be right down the street from Molly Muldoon's. They walked there, got a table in the back, and both had a steak feast that was so good it kept talking to a minimum. It wasn't until dessert that they really started up again.

"You want to go back to Molly's after this for another beer?" Roper asked.

"Why not? We really didn't get a chance to talk with any of those girls, did we?"

"We did not," Roper agreed. "I don't know who was prettier, the girls working the floor, or the girls on stage."

"Then we definitely have to go back and take a good look at both," Clint said.

They finished their pie and coffee, argued over who should pay the bill and left. Roper won the argument, but Clint was buying the next two rounds of drinks.

***

"Just in time for the showgirls, gents," the bartender said, as they reentered Molly Muldoon's. "First round's on the house."

"It's not our first round," Clint said.

"It's your first round this visit," the man said. "Now watch the show and see if you like it better, this time."

They turned to watch . . .

***

It wasn't any better.

Oh, it was just as good for 7 of the girls, but the 8th girl—the one they had heard called "Nell,"—had been allowed to dance again, and if anything, was worse than before.

Clint and Roper winced as they watched her try to match the other girls' movements, but to no avail. She was hopelessly out of her depth.

When the show was over Clint and Roper turned to the bar and picked up their beer mugs.

"So?" the bartender asked.

"Fine," Clint said. "It was fine."

"Okay," Roper said.

"That's all?" The man was obviously disappointed by their reactions.

"Well . . . seven of the girls were really good," Clint said, "but . . . who's that one on the end?"

"Oh, don't even watch her next time," the bartender said. "She's not a regular girl. She's only in there for tonight."

"So what does she really do?" Roper asked.

"That I don't know," the bartender said. "Lou knows all about the girls."

"Is Lou a dancer?" Clint asked.

"No," the man said, "she used to be. But now she just hires the dancers, and sort of mothers them."

"So she's an older woman," Roper said.

The bartender got a look on his face.

"Don't ever let her hear you say that!" he warned.

Chapter Five

Clint and Roper spent the rest of the night getting to know the girls who were working the floor. They met Gina, Ella, Vikki and Mary. When they tried to talk to them about the dancing girls, they all bristled.

"Why do you want to know about them?" the red-haired Ella demanded.

"Yeah, you have us here," blonde Mary complained.

"Those dancers are stuck up, anyway," the dark-haired Gina said. "They wouldn't even talk to you."

"That's right!" the other dark-haired—but short, not long—Vikki chimed in.

"Sorry, girls," Roper said. "We were just curious. No offense meant."

Some of the girls had to leave and serve other customers, but promised to be back. Meanwhile, Ella stayed with them. She was a tall and lean redhead, her hair worn long with freckles across the bridge of her nose. Both Clint and Roper knew that redheads tended to have freckles everywhere.

Everywhere.

"Come on," Roper said, "tell us about that girl on the end. She's lucky she didn't fall over."

"Her!" Ella said. "We've all been wonderin' about her. We don't know how she got a job dancing here. Lou must be losin' her touch."

"All right, then," Clint said, "tell us about this mysterious Lou.

"Lou?" Ella asked. "What's mysterious about her. She was a saloon girl, a dancer, and now she just hires dancers."

"That's all she does?" Clint asked.

Ella shrugged. "No, she also lays out their dance routines for them."

"Is she an older woman?" Roper asked.

"Oh, yeah," Ella said. "She's gotta be . . . forty."

Both Clint and Roper were over forty. Surely, the girl must have realized that.

"Forty's old for a woman," Ella added, as if reading their minds. "For a man it's just a number."

"Well," Clint said, "you won't have to deal with that number for a good long time."

"I'm twenty-eight, already," Ella said. "One of the oldest girls working the floor."

"Really?" Roper asked. "I would've guessed you weren't any older than . . . twenty-three or four."

"You're sweet," she said, putting her hand on his chest. "What's your name?"

"Talbot Roper," he said.

"That's an unusual name," she said. "What do I call you?"

"You can call me Tal."

"Tal," she said. "I like that." She didn't bother to ask Clint his name. Roper had already won her over with his comment about her age.

"I'm going to take a walk around," Clint said.

"You go ahead," Ella said. "I'll keep your friend company."

"I'm sure you will," Clint said, and moved away.

***

He walked around the room, catching snatches of conversation from the tables, men talking about their jobs, their families, and the girls on stage and on the floor. He thought about going into the gambling room, maybe playing a few hands of poker, but it was getting late. If he got involved in a good game, it could go on for hours, even days.

He found himself near the stage when a few of the dancing girls came through the curtain, talking amongst themselves. They smiled at him as they went by, pretty young girls without the make-up and fancy dresses they had been wearing on stage. They sidestepped a table of men who were trying to grab them and, laughing, moved on.

He was about to move on as well when the curtain parted, and another girl came out—the clumsy girl on the right. She was wearing a simple shirt, and boots. She didn't look happy. He wished he knew what to say to her to make her feel better. He was sure that after the second time on stage, she had been fired.

Before he could find any words of solace for her, however, she walked past him. But she couldn't sidestep the table of grabbing hands the way the other dancers had. She couldn't even execute that little dance move.

"Hey, lookee here," one of the men said, "it's that clumsy little gal."

"Jesus, girlie, who told you to be a dancer?" one of the other men laughed.

"Mebbe she's got some other talents, huh?" the third man at the table said. "You wanna come back to our hotel with us, Missy? Show us what you got?"

"Omigod," she said, struggling to get one of the men's thick arm from around her slim waist, "why would I want to go anywhere with you three? I can already see what you've got and I'm not impressed."

Clint thought that her speech was entirely Eastern, probably New York or Philadelphia.

"Now let me go!" she said, and slapped the man's face.

"You bitch!" the man holding her swore. He yanked her into his lap and started to put his hand under her skirt. That was when Clint stepped in.

"There you are, Nell!" he said, loudly.

All three of the players stopped and looked up at him.

"Who're you?" the man holding Nell demanded.

"Me?" Clint asked. "I should ask you who you are, and why do you have my wife in your lap?"

"Your wife?"

"That's right," Clint said. "I told you, Nell, not to come to these places. You never know what types you'll run into."

She stared at him for a moment, then started to play along. She wriggled free of the man and stood up from his lap.

"I know you told me, honey. I'm sorry I didn't listen."

20

The three men were staring at Clint and Nell together, wondering what was going on.

"Hey, wait a minute—" the man who'd been holding her said. He got up, but Clint pushed right up to him.

"Like I said," he told the man, "the lady's my wife. You got a problem with that?"

The man looked into Clint's eyes and immediately backed down. And the gun on Clint's hip helped, too.

"Naw, naw," he said, "I got no problem."

"What about you fellows?" Clint asked. "Got a problem?"

"Nope," one man said, and the other just shook his head and looked into his beer.

"Come on, dear," Clint said, taking Nell's arm, "let's go home."

"All right, honey," she said, like a good little wife.

Chapter Six

"That was amazing!" Nell exclaimed, as they got outside. "They believed us."

"Why wouldn't they believe us?" Clint asked. "Don't I look like I could have a lovely young wife like you?"

"Oh," she said, thinking she had insulted him. "No, no, I didn't mean that. I just—oh, you're teasing me."

"Yes, I am," he said. "Did you get fired?"

"Well, sort of," she said.

"How do you sort of get fired?"

"Well, I didn't really work there."

"You'll have to explain that."

"Since you saved me," she said, "I'd like to buy you a drink, or a coffee, and explain."

"Do you know a place near here for coffee?"

"Yes," she said, "right between here and my hotel The Old West Inn."

"Lead the way, then," he said. "By the way, wife, my name's Clint Adams."

She stared at him, for a moment, then said, "My name's Nellie Bly, and you just made my day, Clint Adams."

***

She led him to a small café, that had tables out in front, as well as inside. When the waiter asked if they'd like to sit outside she immediately told him they'd prefer a table against the back wall. That was when he was dead certain she had recognized his name.

"So, Nellie Bly," he said, when they both had coffee, "what's your story?"

"My story can't be as interesting as yours, Mr. Gunsmith," she said.

"My story hasn't changed in years," Clint said. "I'm more interested in yours. What did you mean when you said you really didn't work at the Emporium?"

"I'm a journalist," she said. "I work for *The New York World* in New York."

"I thought you might be from New York."

"Actually, I was born in Pennsylvania, but I live and work in New York now. I'm out here writing a story on the lives of these showgirls in the dancehalls."

"Ah," Clint said, "so you were looking for experience."

"I had to go undercover. The only problem is, I can't dance."

"I never would have known."

"You're such a liar!" They laughed. "No, only Lou. She pretended to hire me, knows who I really am. She made it look like she hired me, but after tonight she said she had to fire me, or the girls would've known something was up."

"So then I guess your story is dead?"

"Oh no," she said, "I have a lot of material already, and I can still talk to the girls after tonight. No, I'm going to write it, that's for sure."

"And is this the kind of story you want to write?" Clint asked. "It seems kind of . . . light."

"It is," she said. "I'm working my way up to something a lot darker."

"Like what?"

Well," she said, leaning in as she warmed to her subject, "I want to do a story on insane asylums."

"Insane as—why would you want to do that?"

"Because," she said, "they're terrible, horrible places, and I want to prove that they do more harm than good."

"That does sound darker," Clint said. "How are you going to get your information?"

"That's the really dark part," she said. "I want to go undercover as a patient."

"As a patient? That not only sounds dark, it sounds dangerous."

"I can't let that stop me."

"You're a brave girl, Nellie Bly."

"I just have to convince my editor."

"I'm sure you will."

She sat back and smiled at him. "And could I convince you to let me interview you?"

"I've done too many newspaper interviews," he said. "No more for me. You'll have to stick to your dancehall girls and insane asylums."

"Well," she said, "I had to ask."

***

After coffee they stepped outside. It was late, but people were still strolling by, many couples walking arm-in-arm. Clint figured a lot of them were either walking away from or to Molly Muldoon's.

"Oh, hey," he said, "is Molly Muldoon really a man?"

"Yeah," she said, "big belly and a lot of hair. And I mean, all over his body. Not that I—I mean, it sticks out of his shirt. I haven't actually seen his whole body . . ."

"I get it," he said. "How about if I walk you to your hotel?"

She slid her arm into his. "I thought you'd never ask."

Chapter Seven

Clint woke the next morning in his hotel room with a warm hip pressing against his. He opened his eyes and took a look. A girl with chunky breasts and butt was lying next to him, so he knew it wasn't Nellie Bly. But for the life of him he couldn't remember who it was.

He thought back to the night before. He had walked Nellie Bly back to her hotel and made sure she got inside safe and sound. He didn't even try to kiss the young journalist. He liked her, and didn't want to do anything to offend her.

He then went back to Molly Muldoon's. Ah, okay, it was coming back. Roper was still there talking to the long, lean redhead, Ella, and as Clint approached them Ella grabbed him and said, "Somebody wants to meet you!"

"Oh? Who?"

It was the woman who was lying next to him.

She opened her eyes and smiled at him.

"Good morning, Clint."

"Good morning, Lou."

Lou Kendrick was the woman who hired dancers, and who had fired Nellie Bly that night. She was the woman Ella had said was "old," but at 40 she was still lovely, just a little thick through her breasts and butt. No longer a dancer, herself, she "trained" dancers—according to her—and did not "mother" them.

And she told him if he took her back to his room with him she'd show him what a "mother" she wasn't.

And she had.

As soon as they entered the room she was tearing his clothes off him, and then her own. She pushed him down on the bed, mounted him and quickly stroked his cock to hardness and sat on it. After that she rode him hard until her entire body shuddered and she bit her lip to muffle a scream.

"I'm sorry about last night," she said, placing her hand on his belly.

"What's to be sorry about?" he asked.

"Well," she said, "I practically raped you. I just needed a hard, fast fuck."

"That's what you got."

"Yeah," she said, "but what about you?"

"What about me?"

"Looks like you're still interested," she said as she took his cock in her hand. It was semi-hard and getting harder by the second.

"Well," he said, "I have to admit you do still have my interest."

"Let me see what I can do about that."

She slithered down until she was between his legs, kissed the insides of his thighs while fondling his balls, then found his erection with her lips and tongue. She kissed it, licked the length of it until she had it good and wet, and then swooped in to take him into her hot mouth. He lifted his butt off the bed as she began to suck, and she took that as a sign to slide her hands beneath there and cup his ass cheeks. She continued to suck him that way until he let out a great groan and exploded into her mouth . . .

***

He watched her get dressed, a handsome woman with a body once made for dancing, now made for a man's bed.

"I'm sorry to run," she said, "I have so many things to do today."

"I understand."

She came back to the bed and kissed him soundly.

"We haven't even had a chance to know each other," she said. "Will you come by tonight? I can have a drink with you between performances."

"I'll be there."

She smiled happily and breezed out the door.

In minutes he was asleep.

***

When he woke he stretched, feeling both rested, and pleasantly exhausted. But then, instead of thinking about Lou, he started to think about Nellie Bly. What she said about going undercover in an insane asylum sounded way too dangerous for a girl like her. She couldn't have been more than twenty-three or four. He wondered if her editor would even let her do that?

The Show Girl

When he and Lou had separated from Roper and Ella the night before, Clint and the detective agreed to meet for breakfast in the lobby of his hotel. The Denver House had a fine restaurant of its own, and they intended to make use of it.

He washed off and got dressed, but when he left the room he still had the scent of Lou in his nostrils. He hadn't had a chance to do some of the things he wanted to do to her—like burying his face in her pussy, which was something he really enjoyed. He hoped she'd be able to come back to his room with him again later that night. One more time was all he needed to satisfy both that urge, and her needs, at the same time.

He went downstairs to meet Roper.

Chapter Eight

Roper was waiting in the lobby, looking extremely re-laxed.

"You and Ella get along last night?" Clint said.

"Great!" Roper said. "You and Lou."

"She left early this morning," Clint said.

"That's always a good sign."

"That she left early?" Clint asked.

"That she left."

They walked into the Denver House dining room and got a table in the back with no trouble. It didn't matter how long Clint was away, when he returned the staff always remembered who he was, and saw to his every need.

After Roper ordered ham-and-eggs and Clint steak-and-eggs, they each settled back with a mug of coffee.

"What'd you think of the Emporium last night?" Roper asked.

"Very impressive," Clint said. "I didn't get a chance to look in their store, though. Did you?"

"No," Roper said. "I was a little more interested in other parts of the place."

"Like Ella's parts, you mean?"

"Exactly."

"Did you count freckles?"

"I lost count somewhere along the way," Roper admitted.

Breakfast was served and they both tucked into their plates with gusto, having worked up an appetite.

"So how long do you intend to stay?" Roper asked.

"Just a few days," Clint replied. "Long enough to relax, but not long enough for you to get me involved in one of your cases."

"I told you," Roper said, "I have no cases now."

"Well, that situation won't last."

"God, I hope not," Roper said. "I not only have to eat, but I might die of boredom."

"Well, give me a couple of days of your time and then you can take all the cases you want."

"I'll see what I can do," Roper promised.

***

After breakfast they left the hotel. Roper stopped just outside the front entrance and apologized.

"I'm sorry, but I do have a meeting to go to. But I promise I won't take a case until after your gone."

"Look," Clint said, "you do what you've got to do when it comes to your business. Don't worry about me. I met an interesting gal last night and I want to check on her."

"Would that be Lou?"

"No," Clint said, "her name's Nellie Bly. She was the dancer on the end who couldn't keep up? Turns out she's a journalist doing a story on dancehall girls."

"So that explains it," Roper said. "She was terrible."

"And she knew it."

"So she got fired?"

"Yes, Lou said she just couldn't keep her on."

"And what about her article?"

"She's still going to write it, but she also wants to do something more serious."

"Ah," Roper said, "like interview you."

"I told her no," Clint said, "but then I thought . . . why not let her interview you? You've got interesting things to tell her."

"Look," Roper said, "if you want me to let her interview me, I'll do it."

"That's great, Tal!" Clint said. "I appreciate it. I'll let her know today."

"Just let me know when and where she wants to do it," Roper said, "and I'll be there."

"I'll meet you back here tonight for dinner before we go to the Emporium again."

"I'll be here."

They shook hands and parted company.

Chapter Nine

Nellie Bly's hotel, The Old West Inn, was far less expensive than the Denver House, where Clint was staying. Nellie had explained to him the night before that she was paying her own way to write her article. That meant she had to be careful how she spent her money.

The hotel was run down, and the neighborhood matched.

He thought she was very brave to be doing what she was doing. But he thought her courage was going to get her in trouble if she went through with her plan to do the insane asylum exposé.

He entered the lobby, which was empty except for a tired looking whore who was sitting on a ratty divan. She perked up when she saw Clint enter.

"Lookin' for a good time, Mister?" she asked, hopefully. She probably wanted nothing more than to lie down on a bed and let some man have his way while she rested.

"No, thanks," Clint said, "I'm already looking for a girl."

"I'm a girl," she said.

"Obviously," he said, "but I'm looking for a certain girl. Sorry."

She shrugged and leaned back again.

Clint walked to the front desk.

"Sorry about that, Mister," the young man said. "That's Evie. She gives the manager free pokes, and he lets her work the lobby."

"Sounds like a good deal for both of them."

"Are you lookin' fir a room?" the young man asked. He looked to be in his early twenties, very fresh and clean for someone working in that atmosphere.

"No, I'm looking for Nellie Bly's room."

"Oh, Miss Bly," the clerk said. "Uh, can I ask what you want with her?"

"We're friends," Clint said.

"Well," the clerk said, "I'm friends with her, too, and I'm kinda watchin' out for her while she's here."

Clint had a feeling the clerk wanted to be more than just friends with Nellie.

"Well, I'm glad somebody's watching out for her," Clint said. "I was kind of worried about her staying here."

"You don't got to worry," the clerk said. "I'll look out for her 'til she leaves."

"My name's Clint. If you go up and tell her I'm here, she'll tell you it's okay to give me her room number."

"I think I'll do that, then," the clerk said. "I'll be right back."

Clint remained at the desk while the clerk ran up the stairs. Suddenly, he was aware that the whore, Evie, was standing next to him.

"You friends with Nellie?" the woman asked.

"I am."

"She's a sweet kid," Evie said. "That Jimmy, I think he's in love with her."

"Looks like it to me."

"She lets me sleep in her room sometimes, when she ain't there. Ain't that a nice thing for her to do?"

"It sure is."

"Usually, the only time I get to use a bed is with some fella who wants a poke."

"What about when you go home?" Clint asked.

"What home?" the woman asked. "This hotel lobby is my home."

The clerk returned and the whore went back to her divan.

"Okay, Mister," Jimmy said, "she said she knows you, but instead of you goin' up, she's gonna come down."

"That's fine."

Clint walked over to the divan and asked Evie, "Mind if I sit?"

She eyed him for a moment, and he could see that behind the face paint she was about forty-five years old.

"Got a dollar?" she asked.

"I've got two," he said.

She smiled. "Have a seat, then."

She slid over and he sat, giving her two dollars.

"Thanks, Mister. I usually gotta spend two hours on my back for this."

"Glad to help," he said.

"Of course," she added, "for you . . ."

"I'll keep that in mind."

Nellie Bly came down the steps, waved at Jimmy, and walked over to where Clint was sitting.

"Hi, Evie," she said.

"Hello, Nell. This fella yours?"

"Yes, he is," Nellie said, grabbing Clint's arm and pulling him to his feet. "But you can have my room for the afternoon, if you want."

"Do I?" Evie said, standing up.

"Here's the key," Nellie said. "Leave it with Jimmy when you're done."

"Gee, thanks, Nellie," Evie said. "You know, your fella here gave me two dollars, and I didn't even hafta do nothin' for it. He's a helluva nice guy."

"I know it. See you, Evie."

She dragged Clint to the front door and out. On the street she released his arm.

"Good-morning!"

"Good-morning," he said. "You've got yourself a couple of friends, there. In fact, I think Jimmy's in love with you."

"He's not in love with me," Nellie said, "he just wants for free what Evie charges men for."

"He told me Evie gives it out free to the hotel manager," Clint said.

"That's probably true," she said. "The manager is a pig. So what brings you here? You ready to let me interview you?"

"No, but I've got somebody else you'll want to interview, even though you probably never heard of him."

"Try me."

"Talbot Roper."

"He's a private detective here in Denver," Nellie said.

"How do you know that?"

"He's very well known. I've read about him."

"He's a friend of mine, and he's willing to let you interview him while you're here."

"That sounds great!" she said. "Thanks. I guess if I can't interview you, that's the next best thing."

"Better," Clint said. "He's much more interesting than I am."

"I doubt that," she said. "So, how would you like to buy a starving journalist some breakfast?"

"It would be my pleasure," he said, extending his arm so she could take it, again.

***

In the hotel lobby Evie walked over to the front desk and showed Jimmy Nellie's key.

"You wanna come on up for a poke, Jimmy?" she asked. "That feller already paid for it."

"No, thanks, Evie," he said. "You better just keep it warm for Mr. Yates."

Evie made a face at the mention of the hotel manager's name.

"I'd much rather have a clean young man like you than a dirty old timer like him," she said. "Come on, Jimmy. I'll bet you got a nice, big, clean tallywacker on ya. I'll do things to you that you ain't even heard of, before."

Jimmy looked at the whore, wondered if he'd get some kind of disease if he took her up on her offer.

"Maybe another time, Evie," he said. "Go on up and get some sleep."

Chapter Ten

Clint took Nellie out of that neighborhood before finding someplace to buy her breakfast.

"Nothing for you, sir?" the waitress asked, after Nellie had ordered.

"Just coffee," he said. "Thanks."

"You already ate breakfast?" Nellie asked.

"Yes," he said. "As a matter of fact, with Talbot Roper. That's when I convinced him to be interviewed by you. All we need is a time and place," Clint said.

"Well," Nellie said, "since I don't have any more re-hearsals at the Emporium, I'm open."

"Okay," Clint said, "how about tomorrow morning in his office?"

"That sounds good to me."

"All right, then," he said. "That gives you all day and night to come up with your questions."

"How personal can I get?" she asked, as the waitress poured them each coffee.

"That's going to be up to you and him."

"And what will you be doing?" she asked.

"I'm not sure," he said. "Probably walking around the city, trying to decide what my next destination should be."

"You don't have anywhere to go?" she asked.

"Not right now," he said.

"No jobs, nobody to help?" she stared at him. "Yes, I know a lot about you, Clint. All the things I've read started to come back to me last night."

"I see," he said. "Well, as it happens, no, I don't have any jobs or anyone to help, at the moment."

"And nobody to get vengeance against?"

"Now, you can't believe everything you've read, Nellie. Or do you prefer being called Nell?"

"Whatever you like," she said. "You're changing the subject."

"That's because you're trying to interview me," he pointed out.

She looked down sheepishly and said, "Guilty."

The waitress came with her breakfast and they fell quiet while she served it.

"Anything else?" she asked the couple.

"No, thank you," Nellie said. "I'm fine."

"Well, let me know." The waitress was middle-aged, but the look she gave Clint certainly indicated that her juices had not stopped flowing.

"She likes you," Nellie said.

"She doesn't know me."

"But she'd like to."

"Eat your breakfast."

***

They chatted while she ate, mostly Clint deflecting questions, and asking her how it was being a dancehall show girl for a while?

"It was both hard work and fun," she said. "And I learned a lot about how the girls get along."

"Do they?"

"Some of them," she said. "The ones who don't feel they're being competed with. And then there are the saloon girls?"

"What about them?"

"They don't like the dancers," she said, "and the dancers don't like them."

"Isn't Lou in charge of all the girls?" Clint asked.

"No, just the dancers," she said.

"Well, the dancers are the main attraction, aren't they?" he asked her.

"I don't think so," she said. "I think the whiskey and beer and gambling are way ahead of the girls—all the girls."

"What about that store they have?" Clint asked. "What's that about?"

"They thought that people would come in and want to buy things they could take away with them to remember the place," Nell explained. "It was something new they thought would work, but it's not."

"I'm not surprised," Clint said. "Who wants to go into a saloon and go shopping? You do that in a mercantile store."

"They're not ready to give up," she told him. "Somebody's coming in from one of the Denver newspapers to write about it."

"And when are you heading back to New York to write your story?"

"I was hoping to be dancing a little longer," she said. "Now I'll have to go and buy a ticket. Probably day after tomorrow. Thanks to you I have an interview to conduct tomorrow."

"Right," Clint said. "Maybe this interview will convince your editor that you're a serious journalist and you won't have to do that insane asylum thing."

"Oh, I'm doing that," she said. "No doubt. I'm going to make all the arrangements when I get back."

"That sounds too dangerous, Nell."

"I know it'll be hard, but it'll also be worth it."

"Well," he said, "I guess all I can do is wish you luck."

"If I have any trouble," she said, "I'll just call for you. We're friends now, right?"

"Definitely," Clint said. "We are friends."

Months later Clint would remember this conversation.

***

Talbot Roper and Clint Adams put Nellie Bly on a train two days later. She kissed them both on the cheek while saying good-bye.

"She's a smart girl," Roper said.

"She is that," Clint agreed, "but I'm thinking she just may be too smart for her own good."

"The insane asylum story?" Roper asked.

Clint nodded.

"I tried to talk her out of it," Roper said.

"So did I, but she's determined to go through with it."

"Then there's nothing we can do but hope for the best," Roper said.

Clint had his horse, the Darley Arabian, Eclipse, just outside the station, and said good-bye to Roper there. He knew he'd be hearing from and seeing his friend again, but he fervently hoped he'd never hear from Nellie Bly again, because that would probably mean she was in trouble.

Chapter Eleven

3 months later . . .

Clint had returned to Labyrinth, Texas—the closest thing he had to a home—a couple of weeks before, thinking he would stay long enough to recover from his most recent travels. He knew that the misadventures were part of his travels, and the only way to avoid them would be to put down roots. But that was something he was just not ready to do.

Part of the most recent experiences were not one, but two bullet wounds. Neither was very serious, but he did have a sore left arm. He was determined not to leave Labyrinth until he was fully healed.

He had one friend in Labyrinth, a man there who would never leave. Rick Hartman owned Rick's Place, the town's largest casino and gambling hall. Clint didn't know many of the other townspeople. He mostly got to know bartenders and saloon girls who worked for Rick, and invariably, whenever he returned, they were gone and others had taken their place. And the reason for the friendships with Ricks' employees was that they had something in common with Clint. None were ready to put down roots.

During the past two weeks he had made friends and gotten to know a gal named Dawn Reade. Rick had hired her several months before, and since the saloon owner already had a girl warming his bed. He and Dawn had maintained a boss/employee relationship.

When she saw Clint, however, she was immediately interested, and so was he. She was in her early 30's, blonde, busty, smart and pretty. Those were five things Clint really liked in a woman.

He rolled over in the morning as his third week in Labyrinth started and reached down her naked back to her juicy butt.

"Mmmm," she said, as he ran a finger down the cleft between her cheeks, "I love the way you wake me up in the morning."

"I love the way you wake up in the morning," he said. "Always bright-eyed, never bleary."

"And you," she said, sliding her hand over his thigh, "always ready." She grasped his hardening cock.

"That's because you're always beautiful."

"You should have seen me," she said, moving over and putting her chin on his chest, "when I was twenty. I was a goddess."

"No," he said, "I can't imagine that you've been more beautiful at any time of your life than you are right now."

"Oh, you're a sweet man," she said, "and a smooth talker. And do you know where else you're smooth?"

"Where?"

She ran her finger up the underside of his hard penis. "Right here."

When she got to the point just below the head, his penis jerked and she laughed. She kissed his chest, his stomach, and his thighs, then took his cock into her mouth.

He loved the way she woke him up, too . . .

***

Dawn left Clint's room to go and get ready for her day. Clint slept another hour after she left, then got up and dressed. There were two places in town Clint would eat breakfast. One was his hotel dining room, and the other was at Rick's Place. Rick had a man who cooked for him in the morning, but that was it. He didn't serve any food at his place. It was all about drinking and gambling there.

Clint walked to Rick's Place and knocked on the locked front door. It was opened by Clarence, a middle-aged bartender he had only met when he got to town two weeks ago.

"Come on in, Mr. Adams," Clarence said. "You're just in time."

As Clint entered he could smell the steak-and-eggs cooking.

"Good-morning!" Rick greeted, good-naturedly.

Clint walked to the table and sat across from his friend while Clarence poured him some coffee.

"Thanks, Clarence."

"Breakfast in two minutes," the bartender said.

"How are you healing?" Rick asked.

"Good," Clint said. "Not walking with a limp, anymore. And less pain in the arm."

45

"You're gettin' old," Rick said. "I've never known you to take two bullets so close together."

Clint had been shot 10 or 12 times in his life. It was unavoidable. But Rick was right. Never this close together.

"I'm no older than you are," he said.

"I know it," Rick said. "I'm gettin' old, too."

Clarence came out with two plates loaded down with steak, eggs, and potatoes. He set them down.

"Biscuits comin' right out."

"With food like this," Clint asked, "why don't you open a restaurant?"

"Cooks come and go," Rick said. "I'd never be able to keep up these standards."

"Too bad," Clint said.

"If I did open a restaurant would you stay around here longer?" Rick asked. "Maybe put down roots, become my partner?"

"Not a chance," Clint said.

"Why not?"

"I'm just not ready for any of that."

Rick shrugged. "I thought maybe gettin' shot twice—"

"—would push me in that direction? No," Clint said.

"Doesn't your butt get sore from all the riding?"

"Sometimes," Clint said, "but a few days out of the saddle usually fixes that."

"What about Eclipse?" Rick asked. "He's gettin' a little long in the tooth, too, isn't he? After all, you knew when to put Duke out to pasture."

"Eclipse still has a few miles in him," Clint said. "I was lucky that he was able to replace Duke. I don't know that I'll get that lucky, again."

"Then maybe that's when you'll give up the trail, huh?" Rick asked.

Clint cut into his steak and asked, "Why are you harping on this subject, this morning?"

"It's been nice havin' you here the past two weeks, is all," Rick said.

"Well," Clint said, "let's stop talking about it and eat, huh?"

Rick picked up his knife and fork as his answer.

Chapter Twelve

They were having one last cup of coffee when somebody knocked on the front door. Clarence went and opened it, talked with someone, then closed it.

The bartender came right over to the table and held something out to Clint.

"This just came for you, Mr. Adams."

Clint took the telegram from him.

"Uh-oh," Rick said. "This is never good."

"What isn't?"

"You gettin' a telegram here, and in the mornin'."

Clint shook his head, opened the telegram and read it.

"Bad news?" Rick asked.

"Well," Clint said, refolding it, "not good."

"I told you," Rick said. "Somebody lookin' for help?"

Clint nodded, cutting into his steak, again.

"Well," Rick said, "are you gonna keep me in suspense?"

"Nellie Bly."

"That young journalist you told me about?" Rick asked. "What does she want, an interview? Couldn't take no the first time?"

Clint nodded.

"What is her problem?"

"I told you about that insane asylum story she was going to work on?"

"And I told you I thought _it_ was insane."

"Right. Well, she says she went ahead and now she's in trouble. I'm the only one who can help her."

"And why's that?" Rick asked.

"Apparently, I'm the only one who would believe her."

"So, she wants you to come to New York?"

"No," Clint said, "she's in St. Louis, says she'll stay there as long as she can. If they find her before I get there she'll have to run again."

"So when are you leavin'?" Rick asked.

"Right after breakfast."

"Are you gonna tell Dawn?"

"No," Clint said, grinning, "you are."

"Oh, thanks a lot," Rick said.

***

Clint finished his breakfast with Rick, walked directly to the livery, saddled Eclipse and headed for St. Louis, hoping that Nellie Bly would still be there.

***

In St. Louis, Nellie Bly was going on her second week, staying in a small, rundown hotel just off Laclede's Landing, not far from the river. It was called The Atwater.

She should have remained in her room day and night, but she couldn't. After being in the insane asylum she couldn't stand being in small, confined spaces.

So even though she was afraid somebody was trying to find her and kill her, she started taking walks along the landing and down by the docks. But, she was sure to stay away from the more populated parts of the city.

She took all her meals at a nearby café. To be sure no one would bother her, she dressed in clothing too big for her, and didn't wash it. It both disguised who she was, and kept men away from her.

She had just finished her lunch and gone back to her room thinking about Clint Adams, wondering if he had gotten her telegram. She had told him, in her telegram, not to respond to hers. She didn't want anyone to be able to track it to her. She simply asked him to come. She was looking out the window, watching for him. Instead, she saw two men wearing suits approaching the front door of the hotel. They were overdressed for the neighborhood, and she didn't like it. As soon as they faded from view, which meant they were probably in the tiny lobby, she grabbed her jacket, her bag and ran from the room, up the hallways to the back stairs, and down. She waited until she thought the men might be on the way up, then went out the back door.

***

Two days later, Clint crossed the street to the hotel and entered the small lobby. There was a fat, sweaty man at the front desk, who watched as he approached.

"Help ya?"

"I'm looking for a girl," he told the man, "supposed to have a room here."

"Yeah? What's her name?"

"Elizabeth Cochran." Nellie Bly was her pen name. Her real name was Elizabeth Cochran.

"Oh, Liz," the man said, leaning on the desk. "Sure, she had a room here."

"Had?"

"Yeah," the clerk said, rubbing his chin. "Up until two days ago."

"What happened two days ago?"

"Two men came lookin' for her," the clerk said. "Easterners, from the look of 'em. They went up to her room, but she wasn't there. I haven't seen her since."

"Where'd she go?"

"That's what I'm tellin' ya, Mister," the man said. "She's just gone."

"But she didn't check out?"

"No."

"Did she leave stuff in her room?"

"I ain't looked."

"I'd like to look."

"For a dollar?"

"Sure." Clint gave him a dollar and the man gave him the key. He started up the stairs, then stopped. "The two men, did they say who they were?"

"No,"

"But you told them her room number?"

"They were nasty," the man said. "I wasn't about to risk my neck, ya know?"

"Yeah, I know. Did they have guns?"

"Yeah," the clerk said, touching his armpit, "but worn here, ya know?"

"Yeah, I know." Most likely Easterners, he thought. That was bad. "Okay, thanks."

He went up the stairs.

Chapter Thirteen

The room was empty.

Either Nellie hadn't left anything behind, the two men had taken everything, or the clerk had. He walked to the window, looked out, saw that it overlooked the street in front.

He went back downstairs.

"There's nothing up there."

The clerk shrugged.

"But you knew that when you made me pay a dollar for a look, didn't you?"

"Uh . . ."

"When she didn't come back you went up and took a look," Clint went on. "Now, if she left some things there, you took them, or you saw those two men leave with her things."

The clerk didn't answer.

"Or she took her own things when she left."

"That's probably it."

"Then why the dollar?"

The clerk shrugged. Clint put his hand out. The man dug in his pocket and gave the dollar back.

"If she's been gone two days why haven't you re-rented the room?"

"Ain't nobody come in lookin' for a room."

Clint didn't wonder about that. It was a rundown hotel, on the outside and the inside.

"Okay," Clint said, holding up the bill, "for the dollar, what did the two men say? Exactly to you and each other?"

"They came in, asked about the girl the way you did."

"And you told them."

He nodded.

"You try to get a dollar out of them?"

He nodded.

"And that's when they got nasty."

"Yeah," the clerk said, "they said they'd shove the dollar up my ass. So I told 'em."

"But you didn't tell them you hadn't seen her in a while."

"No, because I did. She came back and went to her room about a half an hour before they got here."

"So if she had been looking out her window she would have seen them."

"Probably."

"Is there a back way out?"

"Yeah, a rear door."

"And she could have gotten to it from upstairs."

"Yeah, there's a stairway in the back."

Clint nodded. That was it, then. Nellie had seen the men from her window, gone down the back stairs and ran off. Who knew where she was now? Or if the two men were still looking for her. And if they were, were they looking for her to kill her, like she thought?

"Okay," He gave the clerk the dollar, headed for the door, then stopped and turned. "What did the men say to each other?"

54

"Not much. They grunted, one of them talked to me, did the nasty threats."

"Did they call each other by any names?"

"No."

"Okay," Clint said, "just tell me what they looked like."

The clerk hesitated, then asked, "For a dollar?"

***

The two men from New York sat in a good restaurant in an affluent section of St. Louis.

"It's been two days," Mr. Monroe said.

"I know," Mr. Daly said.

"So what do we do?"

"We keep looking."

"Is that what you say?" Mr. Monroe asked. "Or are those our orders?"

"Orders," Mr. Daly said.

"Shit." Mr. Monroe frowned.

"Hey," Mr. Daly said, "we're getting paid, aren't we?"

"Yeah, we're getting paid."

"Then finish your lunch and we'll start looking again," Mr. Daly said.

***

Clint had taken a room in a decent hotel on Market Street. Not expensive, but not run down, either. He figured Nellie would be hiding out, and might like to have a better room and a bath when she got there.

He started walking back to his hotel, wondering where she might have run to? She was trying to go unnoticed, that was why she stayed on the Landing, near the water. But now that she had to leave, what was next? He hoped she hadn't gotten tired of waiting for him and left the city.

When he reached his hotel, he stopped in the bar to have a beer. It was early, and the hotel bar was not busy. Where else would Nellie go to hide if Laclede's Landing was now off limits?

He needed to talk to somebody who knew the city, somebody who knew where people who didn't want to be found would go. That could be a lawman or a local detective.

He decided on his next move, finished his beer, and left the hotel.

Chapter Fourteen

Clint found the closest telegraph office and sent a wire to Talbot Roper in Denver. He was asking his friend if he knew a detective in St. Louis, hoping that Roper was still in town to see the telegram. Three months ago, when he had been in Denver with Roper the detective had no cases. That was unusual. It was more than likely he was busy now. So he'd have to go to the law for help, which he didn't really want to do. Not without checking with Nellie, first.

"I'm at the Drury hotel," he told the key operator, handing the man a dollar tip. He said, "There's another one if you bring me the reply."

"Yes, sir!" the young man said. "As soon as it comes in."

"Thank you."

He walked back to his hotel, eyes peeled just in case Nellie was walking the streets. But he reached the lobby without spotting her.

Now he was stuck waiting at the hotel until his reply came in—if one came, at all. He went to the bar and ordered a beer.

***

He was at the very dregs of his beer, trying to decide about another, when the clerk from the telegraph office entered. He looked around, spotted Clint and came running over.

"Here's your reply, sir!"

"And here's your other dollar. Thanks."

"Anytime, Mr. Adams."

The clerk left and Clint read the telegram. Roper had been short and sweet, just the name of a man, and an address. The man's name was John Drake.

Clint called the bartender over.

"Can you give me directions to this address?" he asked.

"Sure thing, Mister," the man said, "but that ain't the best part of town."

"That's okay," Clint said. "I'll be careful."

He listened intently as the man gave him the directions . . .

***

The bartender hadn't been kidding.

The buildings Clint passed as he walked down the street looked as if they'd be blown over by a stiff wind. When he reached the address he wanted, it was a two-story wooden structure that fit in with all the others. He was afraid to knock, for fear he might topple the building, but he did it, anyway.

After a few seconds he knocked again, although not harder.

Eventually, someone came to the door. He heard several locks disengage, and then a man's eye peered at him as the door opened a crack.

"Whataya want?"

"I'm looking for John Drake."

"You found him," the man said. "Whataya want?"

"I need some help finding someone," Clint said.

"And what makes you think I can help you?"

"Talbot Roper told me you're the best in St. Louis for the job."

"Roper?" the man said. "Well, why didn't you say so?"

The door opened all the way and Clint found himself staring at a bandy-legged gent in his 40's who stood about five-seven.

"Where is Roper?" he asked.

"Still in Denver," Clint said. "He sent me this." He handed the man the telegram.

Drake read it, then stared at Clint. "Damn my hide! Are you the Gunsmith?"

"That's right."

"Well, come in, come in!" Drake said. "I heard lots about you from Roper."

Clint stepped inside and waited while the man relocked the door, which took a while. When Drake saw him watching he shrugged and said, "Can't be too careful. Come on, follow me."

Drake led Clint down a dark hallway until they reached a large open room. There was a bed in one corner, but for the most part it looked like a huge work room.

"My office," Drake said.

"You own the whole building?" Clint asked.

"I do."

"What's upstairs?"

"There's living quarters, and a shooting range at the far end of the building. That bed is just so I can collapse on it if I don't wanna go up the stairs. I got some whiskey over here. Care for a shot?"

"Sure, why not?"

Drake went over by the bed, where there was a whiskey bottle on a small table. He poured two shots and carried them back to Clint, handing him one.

"Here's to Talbot Roper," he said. "He saved my ass more than once."

"Mine, too," Clint said, "so I'll drink to that."

They tossed back their whiskey and then Drake took the glasses and set them aside.

"Now," he said, "what can I do for you?"

Chapter Fifteen

"I'm looking for a girl," Clint said. "Her name's Nellie Bly, but she was going by Elizabeth Cochran. She was staying at a flea trap hotel on Laclede's Landing called The Atwater."

"Ugh! Not a good hotel," Drake said. "Makes this dump look like a palace."

"This isn't so bad," Clint said. "Anyway, she's a young journalist for *The New York World* and she's in trouble. She was hiding out there, and sent me a telegram to meet her. Only when I got to the hotel, she was gone. The clerk told me two Easterners came looking for her. I think she saw them and now she's on the run."

"You think she's still in St. Louis?" Drake asked.

"I hope so," Clint said, "or I might never find her."

"So you want me to find her for you?"

"If she's hiding, I don't know where to look," Clint said. "I've been here before, but I don't know the city all that well. So I either want you to find her for me, or help me find her."

"And back your play if you run into those two Easterners," Drake added.

"Right. The clerk said they were nasty, and wore guns in shoulder harnesses."

"I got it. Let's go."

"What, now?"

"You need my help now, right?"

"Right."

"Lemme get my gun and jacket, and we'll be on our way. I got a couple ideas where she might be."

***

"The best way to look is on foot," Drake told Clint, as they walked down the street from his building. "Right now, I'm thinking of a few places down here. If we need to go further, we might need a horse and buggy. Do you have a horse?"

"I left my horse behind," Clint said. "Took the train to get here."

"That's okay," Drake said. "If we need horses, I can get 'em."

As they continued to walk Clint found that his superior height was not helping him keep up with John Drake's quick strides. The smaller man moved very fast.

"Is your girl smart?" Drake asked.

"Very smart."

"Okay, so she'd stay far away from the Landing now that somebody went there looking for her," Drake said. "That's good. That narrows it down."

"What other sections of town are like the Landing?"

"This has become a big city," Drake said. "That means there are a lot of sections where people can go to get away, or hide away. This is also gonna depend on how well your girl knows St. Louis."

"Since she chose to hide here, I'd guess she knew it at least a little."

"Never mind," Drake said. "If she's good-lookin' she'll find somebody to help her."

"I think she's going to stay away from men," Clint said. "All men."

"Okay, good to know," Drake said. "Then she'll accept help from females. Now we got a direction."

"What direction is that?" Clint asked.

"This way!" Drake said, taking off at a fast walk.

Which wasn't exactly what Clint meant.

***

Drake took Clint to two soup kitchens, and two rooming houses, all run by women he knew.

"Yes," a woman at the rooming house said, "we take in girls in trouble. What kind of difficulty is she in?"

"She thinks somebody's tryin' to kill her," Drake said.

"Thinks, or knows?"

"Well," Clint said, "we do know that two men are trying to find her."

"Aw now," the woman said, "I can't have that kind of trouble here."

"So two men in suits, like Easterners, ain't been here lookin'?" Drake asked.

"No," she said, "nobody like that. Besides, Easterners? I wouldn't even talk to them."

"Okay, Angie," Drake said, "thanks."

***

One of the women at the soup kitchen said, "I got a girl here right now, says her husband's tryin' to kill 'er."

"That could just be a story," Clint said. "Where is she?"

"Over there, by the window," the woman said, with a jerk of her chin, "eatin' her third bowl of soup."

Clint looked at the girl the woman was referring to.

"That's not her," Clint said.

"Well," the woman said, "that's all I can do for ya."

"Okay, Simone, thanks," Drake said, and started walking away.

Simone grabbed Clint's arm, gave him a sloe-eyed look. She was in her late forties, looked a little tired, but underneath the simple dress she wore was a solid body that hadn't given up the ghost, yet.

"You get rid of Drake and come on back, sweetie," she said, "and I'll give ya somethin' ta eat besides soup."

He patted the hand that was holding his left arm and said, "I'll keep that in mind, Simone."

She released his arm but he could feel her eyes on him all the way out the door.

Outside Drake asked, "Simone tell you to come back without me?"

"She did, yeah."

"She'll keep her promise, you know," Drake said. "She was a high-priced whore in her day."

"I can believe it."

"Come on, then," Drake said. "We still got some places to look."

Chapter Sixteen

After a couple of more stops Drake took Clint to a saloon that looked as if it catered to the dregs of humanity.

"Hey, Johnny," the bartender greeted. "Ain't seen ya around here in a while."

"Been busy, Hector," Drake said. "Meet my friend Clint."

"Pleased ta meetcha." The bartender was in his 50's, shaped like an old fighter. "What kin I getcha?"

"Two beers, Hector," Drake said.

"Comin' up."

As the bartender went off to draw the beers, Clint looked the place over. Not only was there no sign of Nellie Bly, but there were no women in the place, at all.

"Did you think she'd be here?" Clint asked, as Hector set down two mugs of cold beer.

"Naw," Drake said, picking up his drink, "I was just gettin' thirsty."

Clint realized he was thirsty, too. Walking around the city was not easy work. He drank some of his beer, found it crisp and very cold.

"Wow, that's good," he told the barkeep.

"Thanks."

"Hector, we're looking for a dark-haired girl who sounds like she's from the East," Drake said. "She's lookin' for a place to hide out."

Hector leaned on the bar and shook his head. "Not here, Johnny."

"No, I didn't think so," Drake said. "But if you hear somethin'. . ."

"If I do," the bartender promised, "I'll send ya a message."

He looked at Clint. "Your wife?"

"No."

"Girlfriend?"

"Just a friend," Clint said. "I'm trying to help her, but I've got to find her first."

"She didn't tell ya where she'd be?"

"She did," Clint said, "I went there and she'd gone on the run. Two other men are looking for her, and not to help her."

"Poor kid," Hector said.

"What makes you think she's a kid?"

Hector smiled, revealing some missing teeth that had probably been knocked out in the ring.

"They're all kids to me," he said.

"Okay, thanks, Hector. We'll finish these and be on our way," John Drake said.

"Any time, Johnny." He moved on to the other end of the bar.

"You hungry?" Drake asked.

"Getting there," Clint said. "You want to eat here?"

"Hell," Drake said, "I wouldn't eat here."

"Where then?"

"There's a place nearby."

"Simone's?" Clint asked.

"No, why, you wanna go back to Simone's?"

"I don't think so."

"She'd treat ya real good," Drake said, "and feed you."

"Why don't you go there?"

"She's choosy about who she ruts with these days," Drake said. "No old customers."

"You were one of her customers?"

"Oh yeah," Drake said. "Like I said, she was good."

"Well, I think I'll skip it," Clint said.

"Okay then," Drake said, "finish your beer and then we'll keep lookin'. It's gonna be dark soon. She'll have to find a place to bed down."

"Yeah, she will."

"Might try another hotel, if she's got the money."

"She'll have some," Clint said, "but I don't think a lot."

"Then she'll probably find another flea bag," Drake said. "We got plenty of 'em." He finished his beer and set the empty mug down. "But first we eat."

Clint placed his mug next to Drake's.

"Want me to pay?" he asked.

"Don't worry about it," Drake said, "Hector and me, we got an arrangement."

***

After they left the saloon, Hector the bartender, waved over one of his customers.

"Whataya need?" the skinny man asked.

"Leo," Hector said, "the other day them two fellas who came in lookin' for a girl. Was they Easterners?"

"Yeah, I think they was."

"Do we know where they're stayin'?"

"They said they was stayin' at the Victoria."

"And how much did they say they'd pay for information?" Hector asked.

"A helluva lot!" Leo said. "Whatsamatta with your memory, Hector?"

"I just wanna be reminded," Hector said. "This has gotta be worth betrayin' a friend, ya know?"

"Well," Leo said, "if I remember right, the money they was offerin' for information about the girl was worth betrayin' more than one friend, and your mother!"

"That's what I thought," Hector said. "Why don't you take a run over to the Victoria and ask them two gents to come on by here again. We got some information for them."

"Where the girl is?" Leo asked. "Remember, they wanna know where the girl is."

"Not exactly," Hector said, "but if we help them find the girl, maybe they'll still pay."

Chapter Seventeen

Again, John Drake took Clint to an establishment that looked rundown on the outside, slightly better on the inside. The food, however, was top notch.

"This place should have more customers with food like this," Clint said.

"They're satisfied with the customers they get every day," Drake said. "They do a good business, and don't have to worry about how the place looks."

"So what are we going to be doing after this?" Clint asked, around a mouthful of fried chicken.

"After dark our choices become much different," Drake said. "She's gonna need a place to bed down, especially if she's an Eastern journalist. I can't see any of them sleepin' on the street, especially not a girl. If she's smart enough, she'll find herself a place."

"Well, she's pretty smart," Clint said, "but I think you're right, she wouldn't be tough enough for the street. Not yet, anyway. She's still a little young."

"She was in an insane asylum, ya say?"

"Put herself in there, for research," Clint clarified. "Then when she got out, somebody tried to kill her."

"I wonder what she found out in there that makes her so dangerous?" Drake asked.

"I don't know," Clint said. "I think that was part of what she needed help figuring out. If it was just bad medical practices, I don't think anybody would be trying to kill her to cover that up."

"Could it be she's wrong?" Drake asked. "Imagining that somebody's tryin' to kill 'er?"

"I guess I'll have to try and figure that out when I find her."

"And if you don't find 'er?"

"That's not an option," Clint said. "I'll just keep looking until I do. I mean, I've come all this way."

"I hate to bring this up," Drake said, "but what happens if you find her, and she's dead?"

"Well then," Clint said, "I find whoever killed her."

"Okay," Drake said. "Good enough for me. Let's finish up here and get back to lookin'."

***

Hector looked up as the batwing doors opened and Leo led two men into the saloon. Both were well-dressed; one was tall and the other was short.

"This fellow says you've got some information to sell," Mr. Daly said. He was the tall one.

"And it better be good," Mr. Monroe said.

"Just relax," Mr. Daly told him. "What do you have for us, bartender?"

"Can we settle on a price first?" Hector asked.

"The price is going to depend on exactly what you have to sell," Mr. Daly said.

Hector thought that over, decided that it made sense.

"A coupla fellas was in here lookin' for the same girl you're lookin' for."

"Is that right?" Mr. Daly said. "Who were they?"

"One was a local boy named John Drake," Hector said. "Works as a private detective here in St. Louis. Knows his way around. If he's lookin' for somebody he generally finds 'em."

"And the other man?"

"Don't know him," Hector said. "Drake called him Clint, but that was it."

"Not local?" Mr. Monroe asked.

"Nope," Hector said." Impression I got is he came to St. Louis lookin' for that gal."

"Did they say her name?" Mr. Daly asked.

"Nope," Hector said, "just described 'er."

The two men exchanged a glance.

"That worth anythin' to you?" Hector asked.

Mr. Daly pursed his lips for a minute, then said, "Some, but I'll tell you what would be worth more."

"What's that?"

Mr. Daly looked around, then crooked his finger at Hector to come a little closer . . .

***

Clint and John Drake finished their meal and left the little café. Clint noticed that Drake didn't pay there, either. He must have had the same arrangement with many of the city's business owners.

"Okay, where to?"

"Coupla places I know of where folks bed down when they have no other place to go."

"Walking distance?"

"Pretty much."

They started walking. The streets were dark, with even darker shadows around them.

"Relax," Drake said.

"Easy for you to say," Clint said. "I live my life trying to see inside every shadow."

"Not here," Drake said. "You're with me. Ain't nobody gonna try nothin'."

"I hope you're right," Clint said. "I'm not looking for any trouble."

"Seems to me a man like you has just got trouble followin' him wherever he goes."

"You've pretty much got that right."

"Then you deserve a break," Drake said. "And bein' with me on these streets is it."

"If you don't mind," Clint said, "I'm not going to let my guard down."

John Drake shrugged and said, "Suit yerself."

Chapter Eighteen

John Drake took Clint to two flophouses, which made the flea bag hotels look opulent. Nellie Bly was not in either.

As they left the second one he said, "Jesus, I hope she doesn't end up in a place like that."

"I have another suggestion," Drake said, "but you're not gonna like it."

"What's that?"

"We can start checking the hospitals, and the morgue."

"Let's put that off," Clint said. "If she's in the morgue she's not going anywhere."

"Okay," Drake said.

"Any more of these places?" Clint asked.

"A few," Drake said. "We can get to them tonight."

"And then what?" Clint asked.

"And then we get some sleep and start over tomorrow," Drake answered.

"You got more places to check?"

"Hey," Drake said, "there are lots of alleys, and then I'm sorry to say, but we'll have to start repeating. She could show up someplace we already looked."

"Good point," Clint said.

***

After checking two more flophouses Clint and Drake returned to Drake's building. As they approached a man came out of the shadows, holding his hands out to show that they were empty.

"Dangerous stuff, Leo," Drake said, "coming out of the shadows like that."

"That's why I'm showing my hands, Johnny."

"Hector send you?"

"Yeah, he wants you to come back to his place."

"He's got some information for us?"

"That's what he said. He wants you to come."

"Tonight?"

"Tomorrow night, he said."

"Good," John Drake said. "I want to get some sleep tonight."

"Well . . . okay, I'll tell 'im." He started to leave, then turned back and looked at Clint. "Oh, Hector wanted you to bring your friend."

"This friend?" Drake asked, pointing at Clint.

"That's right."

"Tell him I will," Drake said.

Leo nodded, then turned and disappeared into the shadows.

Drake unlocked the door and they went inside. He poured two glasses of whiskey and handed Clint one.

"Now what was that about?" Clint asked. "If he knew something, why didn't he tell us before?"

"Because he don't know nothin'," Drake said.

"Then why send for us?"

"See, that's the big giveaway," Drake said. "He sent for both of us."

"Meaning?"

"Meanin' it's a trap."

"A trap? But I thought he was a friend of yours."

"I got very few friends, Clint," Drake said. "A friend is somebody who won't sell you for money."

"You think he's getting paid?"

"I think he made a deal with your two Easterners to deliver us," Drake said. "You and me, only he don't know who you are. That's gonna be a big surprise."

"So if he's setting us up for those two men, they don't have Nellie and they don't know where she is."

"Nope," Drake said. "They're lookin' for her just like we are."

"So him asking for me, too, was the big giveaway?"

"Also," Drake said, "setting the meet for tomorrow night, instead of right now. That gives him time to contact the two gents, and gives them time to set the trap."

"What if we go over there tonight—"

"Tonight's no good," Drake interrupted. "We need sleep. Tomorrow will be soon enough. We'll go see Hector nice and early, and then we'll set a trap of our own. It won't help us find your girl, but it might tell us who's tryin' to kill her, and why."

"Roper was right about you," Clint said.

"Roper's right about most things," Drake said. "You can take that bed over there, and I'll go upstairs. We'll get started nice and early."

"Okay," Clint said, "it's your play."

"My city, my play," Drake said. "You got that right."

Drake took his glass and the bottle of whiskey and went up to his living quarters. Clint heard him moving about for a while, but then he settled down.

***

Clint tried to sleep but couldn't.

He got up, lit a lamp and walked around. Drake had a lot of tools, indicating that he was a little more than just a detective. His work area indicated he had skills with his hands, as well.

Clint walked to a front window and looked out. There were no lights close by, but he could see some in the distance. He wondered if anyone over there was able to see the lamp he had lit?

He thought about Nellie Bly. It seemed like the young journalist had definitely gotten herself into a lot of trouble. Once he found her, they'd have to figure how to get her out. But first he and Drake were going to have to plan a way out of the trap that Drake's "friend" had set up for them.

He only hoped that he could trust Drake more than Drake could trust his friend, Hector.

Chapter Nineteen

In the morning, when Drake came back down, Clint was already awake.

"I don't have any food here, so we'll have to go and get some coffee and breakfast," Drake said.

"Suits me," Clint said.

"And then we'll go pay Hector a visit before he opens," the detective went on.

"Do you think he really expects you to walk into a trap?" Clint asked. "Doesn't he know you better than that?"

"Apparently not," Drake said, "or he wouldn't have even sent Leo with the message. I think he's blinded by the money he thinks he's gonna get."

"I'll blind him with something else if he doesn't agree to help us," Clint said.

"Oh, he'll agree," Drake said. "See, he doesn't know who you are, so he couldn't figure that into his plan. Also, he couldn't tell those two, either. So nobody knows who they're dealin' with."

"Well," Clint said, "this is one of the times I won't mind using my name and reputation to scare somebody."

"Really?" Drake said. "You don't make use of it?"

"Not deliberately," Clint said. "It works against me more often than it works for me."

"Well," Drake said, "I guess we'll be testin' that theory out, won't we?"

***

They were in a crowded and rundown café where many of the people seemed to know Drake—who made sure he introduced Clint Adams, "the Gunsmith."

"Can we stop beating that dead horse?" Clint asked.

"If somebody's holdin' the girl," Drake said, "and the word gets around about who it is that's lookin' for her, it might work in our favor."

"I just don't want to shout it from the rooftops," Clint said. "Somebody's going to take a shot at me."

"You really think so?"

"Somebody's always looking to take a shot at me!"

"All right, all right," Drake said, "we'll give it a rest, then."

Clint pushed his plate away. Under other circumstances, he would have enjoyed the breakfast.

"Can we get a move on now?" he asked, impatiently.

"Sure, sure," Drake said, popping the last piece of crisp bacon into his mouth. "Let's go."

***

They left the cafe and walked to Hector's bar, which was closed that early in the morning.

"He lives behind it," Drake said. "Let's go around back."

Clint followed Drake down an alley to the rear of the building. The door was locked, but Drake held his finger to his lips and then kicked the door open so hard it came off its hinges.

The back room of the saloon was a storeroom, but in one corner there was a small bed. Hector had been lying on it, his feet extending past the bottom. As the door shattered he sat up quickly, looking around with wide eyes. Drake was on him before he could get his bearings.

"Hello, Hector," Drake said, getting in the bartender's face.

"Oh, uh, hi, Johnny," the barman said. "What's the idea of breaking my door down?"

"Maybe I should introduce my friend properly," Drake said. "He'll let you know what we're looking for." He pointed at Clint. "This is Clint Adams, Hector . . . the Gunsmith."

"The . . . Gunsmith?"

"That's right," Drake said, "and he understands that you've gone against him, by trying to set a trap for us tonight."

"W-w-w-what? Nooooo . . . the Gunsmith?"

"That's right," Drake said. "The legend of the West. And you're tryin' to help two Easterners trap him."

"No, no," Hector said, looking at Clint with frightened eyes, "I didn't know—"

"That's no excuse," Clint said. "You're trying to help them catch a girl who's a friend of mine. And you're doing it by feeding me and Drake to them, for money."

Hector looked at Drake.

"Did Leo tell you that?" he asked. "He's a liar. You can't trust a thing—"

"You know, Hector," Drake said, putting his arm around the man and tightening the hold, "I used to think I could trust you. I used to think you were my friend."

"I am, I am your friend, Johnny."

Drake slapped Hector on the back of the head and said, "Good, I'm glad to hear it. If you're my friend, then you're gonna help me, right?"

"Right," Hector said, then, "help you with what?"

"Instead of your two Easterners settin' up a trap for us," Drake said, "you're gonna help us set a trap for them. Understand?"

"B-but—"

"But nothing? They were gonna pay you?"

"Uh, yeah—"

"Well," Drake said, "we're not gonna pay you. You know what we're gonna do?"

"What?"

Drake turned to look at Clint.

"You tell 'im."

"It's simple, Hector," Clint said to the bartender, "we're going to let you live."

Chapter Twenty

Later that evening, after dark, Clint and Drake were in Hector's back room. He was behind the bar, waiting for the Easterners to arrive, and turning away customers—although there weren't that many.

"Is he going to stick to the plan?" Clint wondered aloud. "He looks jumpy."

"Oh, he'll stick to it," Drake said, "or he knows we'll put a bullet through his head right from here."

Clint was not nervous about facing the two men who were looking for Nellie Bly, but he was nervous about where Nellie was. She seemed to have gone to ground very convincingly for someone who was not a St. Louis native. On the other hand, why had she chosen St. Louis unless she was familiar with it?

That was something he'd find out when—and if—they managed to find her.

"Okay, what's this?" Drake said.

The batwing doors swung open and several men entered, all wearing holstered sidearms. And then, following behind them, came two men wearing suits.

"This must be them," Clint said.

"And they brought help," Drake said.

Which they hadn't expected.

"I count six, altogether," Drake said.

"Me, too."

They moved back from the doorway and looked at each other.

"Okay, this is your bailiwick," Drake said. "Wild West shootouts are somethin' I ain't familiar with."

Clint knew he was only too familiar with them. These two Easterners had hired four gunnys, without knowing who they were dealing with.

"Maybe when they know who I am they'll all back down," Clint offered.

"How often does that happen?"

"Hardly ever," Clint admitted. "Seems everybody is out for a reputation."

"And killin' you would sure give 'em one."

"Right."

"So maybe," Drake offered "if we get the drop on 'em they'll back down, not even knowing who you are.

"That's possible."

"Then how do we get the drop on 'em?" Drake asked.

They both looked into the saloon again, and saw one of the Easterners pointing toward the back room.

"We better move," Drake said, "looks like they're going to send at least two men back here."

"No," Clint said, "this will work in our favor."

"How?"

"Just listen . . ."

***

Mr. Daly said, "I want two of you in the back room. You other two, go and sit at a table with a beer.

"And us?" Mr. Monroe asked.

"Oh, we're going to be right here at the bar," Mr. Daly said. "When they walk in we'll just look like two customers having a beer."

"You don't think we're going to stick out?" his partner asked.

"Probably," Mr. Daly said. "But we've got every eventuality covered."

Hector shook his head. These men had no idea what they were about to go up against.

Both men bellied up to the bar with beers, and waited . . .

***

Clint approached the batwing doors from outside, hoping that Drake was as good as Roper said he was, and that he was in position.

He stopped just in front of the doors, knowing he had at least 4 men waiting for him inside. But the two Easterners had their guns in shoulder holsters beneath their jackets, not easily accessible. He hoped to be able to count on that.

He went through the batwing doors . . .

***

"Here's the fella who was with Drake," Hector said to the two men.

"And where's Drake?" Mr. Daly asked.

"I don't know," the bartender said. "Maybe he decided not to come."

The two men watched through the mirror as Clint surveyed the room.

"Better not wait," Daly said to Monroe, who nodded.

Both men turned.

***

Clint studied the two men who were seated at separate tables. They looked like every two-bit gun he'd ever faced before. Hopefully, they weren't better than they looked.

As he turned to the bar the two men wearing suits faced him.

"Am I supposed to be surprised?" Clint asked, before they could speak. "You think I didn't know you would be here, and probably with help?"

Mr. Monroe stole a glance at Hector the bartender, who lowered his eyes, then looked at Clint.

"That's all right, sir," Mr. Daly said. "You knew we were coming here, and yet you still walked in alone. That's fine. Gentlemen?" he said to the other two men.

They stood up from their table.

"Maybe, before you tell these two gents to go for their guns, I should introduce myself," Clint said. "Or, better yet, we'll let Hector do it. Hector, tell these nice fellows who I am."

"Yes, bartender," Mr. Daly said, "tell us who we're killing."

"Um, yeah," Hector said, "you should probably know that this fella is Clint Adams."

Mr. Monroe looked at Hector.

"Is that supposed to mean something to us?" he asked.

"Hey," one of the other men said, "we're gonna need a little more money if you want us to go up against the Gunsmith."

Chapter Twenty-One

"Wait, wait," Mr. Daly said, "isn't that some sort of old West legend?" He frowned, as if trying hard to remember. "I would have expected you to be . . . older."

The other two men in the room laughed nervously.

"I'm old enough," Clint said.

"Maybe too old," Mr. Daly said. "Maybe it's time to hang up your guns. You don't know what you're walking into, here."

"I think it's the other way around, friend," Clint said, "and since you now know my name. Maybe I should know yours."

"I'm called Mr. Daly," the spokesman said, "and this is my colleague, Mr. Monroe."

"And these two are hired hands?"

"Exactly."

"And the two in the back room?"

"The two in the—" Mr. Daly started, and then stopped.

Two guns came flying out from the back room and struck the floor. Then John Drake followed.

"These hired hands are out of commission," Drake said.

"Your odds are not as good as you thought, Mr. Daly," Clint said.

"I suppose you're right," Mr. Daly said. "Still, I have a job to do."

"Then let's talk about that," Clint said. "Your job is to catch Nellie Bly and . . . what? Stop her from writing her story? Take her back to New York? Or just kill her?"

"This is presupposing I know who and what you're talking about," Mr. Daly said. "Nellie Bly?"

"If you're not here for that, then why are you here?" Clint asked.

"My friend and I are just having a beer," Mr. Daly said.

"Sorry," Clint said, "Hector's already told us about your plan."

"Hector?" Mr. Daly said, frowning. "Our plan?"

"To bushwhack us," Drake said.

Mr. Daly spoke to Drake without taking his eyes off of Clint.

"I'm afraid I don't know what you're talking about," he said. "My friend and I were just leaving when you arrived."

"And what about these two?" Clint asked.

"And the two in the back room?" Drake added.

Mr. Daly shrugged. "I'm afraid we don't know them."

"What?" one of the men said.

"Hey," the other spoke up, "you can't just—"

"No," Clint said, "they can't. As a matter of fact, if you two want to leave and forget all about this, by all means, go."

The two men exchanged a look and the one said, "Oh, we're goin', Mister."

"Leave your guns on the table," Clint said, as they started to move.

"Our guns?" the one said. "Hey—"

"We're not letting you leave here with your guns," Clint said, "and wait for us outside. You can come back for them later, when we're gone."

The two men exchanged a look, then took their guns from their holsters, set them on the table and headed for the door.

When they reached the batwings one of them turned and said, to Mr. Daly and Mr. Monroe, 'Don't contact us again."

"What about the two in the back?" Drake asked.

"They can make their own decisions," the man said, and left.

"There you go," Clint said. "Now the odds are nice and even, aren't they?"

Mr. Daly spread his hands apart.

"We are not gunmen."

"Maybe not," Clint said. "But you're killers."

"Why do you say that?" Mr. Monroe asked.

"I can tell," Clint said. "I've been dealing with killers most of my life. And you two fit the description."

Mr. Daly looked over at Mr. Monroe. Clint knew that the two had been partners so long they were able to communicate without speaking.

"Don't be stupid," Clint said. "All you have to do is tell me what I want to know, and you can walk out."

"Sorry, Mr. Adams," Mr. Daly said, "but I'm afraid it doesn't work that way."

"Look—"

Both men reached inside their jackets for their guns. Despite the fact they were wearing shoulder rigs, they got their guns out pretty quick.

Just not quick enough.

Clint drew and shot Mr. Monroe in the chest. As the man crumpled, but before he hit the floor, Clint also shot Mr. Daly in the chest.

Across the room John Drake had his gun out, but he was too slow. The action was over.

"Jesus Christ!" Hector shouted.

"Jesus has nothing to do with it," Clint told him, ejecting his spent shells and replacing them.

"I never seen nothin' that fast!" Hector said.

"Neither have I," Drake said, approaching Clint.

"They didn't leave me a choice," Clint told them.

Drake looked down at the two men. "No they didn't."

He bent down and checked them both.

"They're dead," he said.

"The two in the back?"

"Alive."

"Okay," Clint said, "maybe they know something."

"You'll have to wait until they wake up," Drake said.

"Meanwhile," Clint said, "Let's take a look and see if these fellows were carrying anything that might tell us who sent them here."

"Hector," Drake said, bending down with Clint to go through the dead men's pockets, "Two beers."

"Comin' up!"

Chapter Twenty-Two

"Do we need to notify anyone?" Clint asked John Drake over their beer.

"Like who?" Drake asked.

"The law?"

"No," Drake said, "me and the law don't see eye to eye."

"What about the bodies?"

"After we talk to the two in the back room we'll make 'em take the bodies with them. Let them worry about what to do with 'em."

Clint thought about that, then agreed it was a good idea. He didn't particularly want to deal with the local law, either.

"We might as well get to it, then," Clint said.

Drake headed for the back room, taking his beer with him, so Clint did the same.

"These guys look like locals," Drake said, before they went through the door. "How about lettin' me take the lead? You lay back, sip your beer, and look mean. If I need to call you in, I will."

"Okay," Clint said, "you take the lead."

Drake turned to go into the back room, but Clint put his hand on his shoulder.

"What about the bartender?" Clint asked.

"Hector!" Drake shouted. "Lock the doors and don't let anybody in."

"Okay."

"And don't go anywhere!"

"Uh, yeah, all right."

Drake looked at Clint, who said, "All right, I guess."

Drake grinned and went into the back room.

***

They started by waking the two men up, and then tying their hands behind them. Their guns were tossed off into a corner.

"Okay, gents," Drake said, "my name's John Drake, but more importantly, standing behind me is the Gunsmith, Clint Adams."

"Huh?" one man said.

"Aw, he ain't real,' the other said.

"Oh, he's real," Drake said, "and I hope you fellas got paid in advance, because he just killed the two Eastern gents you were workin' for."

"Wha-jeez—" one started.

"And, by the way, if you're lucky," Drake went on, "we'll let you leave, but you're gonna have to take those bodies with you."

"What are we supposed to do with them?" one man asked.

"We don't care," Drake said. "Just get rid of 'em. But first, you have some questions to answer, like, what are your names?"

"I'm Dawson," the first man said.

"My name's Price."

"Price," Drake said, "I've heard of you."

"And I've heard of you, Drake," Price said.

"What the hell were you doin' workin' for these two dudes?" Drake asked.

"They were payin' really well," Price said, "and we didn't know you were involved . . .or him."

"What was the job?"

"Just backin' them up," Price, who had become the spokesman, said.

"Did you know what they were doin' in St. Louis?" Drake asked.

"All they said was that they were lookin' for somebody."

"They didn't say who or why?"

"We got the feelin' it was a girl," Price said, "but that's all."

"And what were you wilin' to do for them?" Drake asked.

"Nothin'," Price said. "Just back their play."

"Whatever it was?" Drake asked. "Like murder?"

"No!" Price said. "We were just supposed to keep them from gettin' killed."

"Okay," Drake said, "who did they work for? Who sent them here?"

"We don't know," Price said. "They just said that we worked for them."

"So you don't know who was payin' the bills for them?"

"No idea."

"I think," Drake said, "if I was gonna work for somebody like these two I'd want a little more information. Price, I'm thinkin' you'd want the same thing. You and your partner."

"Look," Dawson said, "things have been rough, lately. We needed the work."

"That's not a lie," Price said. "Come on, Drake, you know. We're not in demand like you are."

Drake turned and looked at Clint, who just kept sipping his beer.

"Who were the other two guys with you?" Drake asked.

"That was Greg Paulsen and Joey Getz," Price said. "Are they dead, too?"

"No," Drake said, "the Gunsmith gave them the option of leavin' on their own, and they did."

"So just Daly and Monroe are dead?" Price asked.

"That's right."

"You knew their names," Clint said.

"What?" Price said.

Drake stepped aside.

"The two men who hired you, you knew their names."

"Well, yeah," Price said, "when they hired us, they told us their names."

"And who gave them, your names?" Clint asked.

"I think that was Joey."

Now Clint was upset they had let the other two go. Maybe Joey Getz knew more about them.

"Do you know how to contact Joe?"

"Well . . . yeah," Price said.

Clint looked at Drake, who nodded.

Chapter Twenty-Three

They untied Price and Dawson, took them out to the bar so they could see the dead bodies. Then they gave them each a glass of whiskey.

"This is what I want you to do," Clint said to Price. "Tell Joey he's got to come back here to get his gun later today."

"And you'll be waitin' for him?" Price asked.

"That's right. Once you've delivered the message let Hector know. He'll pass it on to us. Right, Hector?"

"Right, Drake, right."

"Are you gonna kill 'im?" Price asked.

"That's not the plan," Drake assured him. "We never should've let him and his partner leave without questionin' them the way we did you."

"We want to find out if Joey knows more about these two than you did," Clint said, "since he's the one who put you together with them."

"What's this all about?" Price asked. Why'd these two have to die?"

"They had to die because they went for their guns," Clint said. "They didn't give me a choice. As for what it's about, that's what we're trying to find out."

Drake gave Price and Dawson their guns.

"You trust us with these?" Price asked.

"I told you who he is," Drake said, indicating Clint, "and you can see what he did, here. If you don't do what he asks, he'll find you."

"Oh, don't worry," Price said, "I'll do what he told me to do. Joey's deserves it for gettin' me mixed up in this."

"Just keep thinkin' that," Drake said. "And don't forget to get rid of these bodies."

"Yeah, yeah," Dawson said, "we'll get rid of 'em."

"Hector," Drake said, "go ahead and open after these bodies are gone. And don't try to cross me again, friend."

"Aw, Drake, it was just the money," Hector said. "We're still friends, right?"

"Just don't make me come back here for anythin' other than a beer,"

"Right, right."

"We'll be back later to make sure Joey got the message."

Clint and Drake left the saloon.

***

"Do you think they'll go along?" Clint asked, when they were outside.

"I think Price and Dawson are scared enough to do what we told 'em to do," Drake sad.

"And Hector?"

"He tried to make a little extra money," Drake said. "He knows he did somethin' wrong."

"You're very understanding."

"Not so much," Drake said. "He just knows if he does it again, I'll kill 'im. You hungry?"

Clint shrugged. "I could eat."

Chapter Twenty-Four

Over a meal—which Clint wolfed down-Drake asked, "Do you ever have a problem eatin' after killin' a man?"

"Or two?" Clint asked. "I used to, in the beginning, but I quickly learned that making me kill them was their fault. Why should that affect my appetite?"

"I suppose that makes sense."

"What about the girl?" Clint asked. "Do you have any more ideas about where to look for Nellie?"

"One or two," Drake said. "We can check them out after we finish eatin'."

"And then go back to Hector's bar," Clint said, "see if Joey got our message."

"Right. By the way . . ."

"What?"

"I agree with Hector," Drake said.

"About what?"

"I've never seen anythin' so fast," Drake said. "Are you the fastest who ever lived?"

"No."

Drake waited for more, and when it didn't come he asked, "Who's faster?"

"I don't know," Clint said, "but I'm sure they're out there."

"So somebody you've never met may be faster," Drake said, pushing it. "What about others that you <u>have</u> met? Bat Masterson? Wyatt Earp? Doc Holliday?"

"Any one of them might have been faster than me, but we never had cause to find out."

"What about Wild Bill Hickok?"

"What about him?"

"I read that you and him were friends."

"That's right, we were."

"Were you in Deadwood with him?"

"No," Clint said, "the last time I saw Bill I was a deputy of his in Abilene."

"Was he fast?"

"He may have been the fastest I ever saw."

"What about the stories that he shot men in the back?" Drake asked.

"I think we're done talking about this, now," Clint said.

"Oh, hey, sorry," Drake said, "I'm just curious. No offense meant."

"None taken," Clint said. "I just don't like talking about the dead."

"Okay, then," Drake said. They were back in the restaurant where he had first taken Clint to eat, so they got up and walked out without paying.

***

"Nellie?"

Nellie Bly heard her name whispered, turned her head quickly. It was Tommy, the boy who had been hiding her in his parent's barn for days, now. They had met on the street, Nellie pretending to be an 18-year-old homeless girl. Tommy was 17, and she could tell that he liked her. She felt bad for lying to him.

"Tommy?"

"Yeah, it's me." He came into the dark barn, carrying a lantern. "I brought you some cold chicken."

"Thanks."

He sat down on the hay next to her and handed her the food wrapped in a napkin. She tore it open and began eating it.

"Did you find out anything that I asked you."

"Yeah, I did," he said. "There's this fella goin' around lookin' for ya. I heard it in a saloon."

"What were you doing in a saloon?" she asked. "You're seventeen."

"You told me you needed information," he said. "I went everywhere tryin' to find it—restaurants, hotels, and saloons."

"Okay," she said, biting into a chicken leg, "what did you find out?"

"This fella's lookin' for you, his name's Drake, John Drake."

"Do you know him?"

"I heard of him," Tommy said. "Everybody has."

"Who is he?"

"A detective, he says," Tommy answered.

"What do you mean, 'he says?'"

"He does other things," Tommy said.

"Does he break the law?"

"Close," Tommy said. "I heard people say he bends the law."

"And why is he looking for me?"

"He's got another man with him," Tommy said, "He's the man that's lookin' for ya."

"And what's his name?"

"I heard it once. Not the whole name, just the first."

She waited, and when he didn't say it she asked, "So, what is it?"

"Clint," Tommy said, "his name's Clint. Do you know him?"

She dropped the chicken onto the napkin and pushed it away.

"I know it," she said. "Come on."

"Where?"

"You have to take me to him."

"To who? Drake?"

"No, the other man," she said. "Clint."

"Who is he?"

"He's Clint Adams, and I asked him to meet me here, in St. Louis."

"Clint Adams . . . The Gunsmith?" Tommy got excited.

"That's right."

"You know him?"

"Yes, I do."

"How?"

"We're friends."

He gave her a disbelieving look.

"You're eighteen, you live on the street, and you're friends with the Gunsmith?"

She put the rest of the chicken aside, turned to face him and took his hands.

"Look, Tommy, I'm going to tell you the truth," she said. "I'm not eighteen, and I'm not homeless. I'm on the run."

"From who?"

"From men who want to kill me."

"Really?"

"Yes, really."

"But why?"

"Because I know something I'm not supposed to know," she said, "and they don't want me to write about it."

"Wow," he said. "Write about it where?"

"In a New York newspaper," she said. "I write for *The New York World*."

"How old are you, really, then?"

"Twenty-four."

"Wow," he said, again. "So the Gunsmith is gonna help you?"

"He's going to save me."

He squeezed her hands.

"I'll save you!"

She stood up.

"That's sweet, Tommy, but you can't. You're just a boy."

"A boy who's been hidin' you," he said, standing, "and feedin' you."

"And I appreciate it," she said. "But now you have to be the boy who takes me to Clint."

She started for the door, but stopped when he said, "I don't want to."

She turned to face him.

"Tommy, if he's out there looking for me, he's going to run into the men who want to hurt me. I have to warn him about what's going on." She walked back to him, took his hand. "I have to find him, and I need your help."

"And then what?" he asked. "You'll go away with him?"

"I'm not going away with him," she said. "I just need his help."

"So he's really your friend?" he asked.

"Yes."

"And that's all?"

"Yes."

She could see he was jealous, and knew she would have to play to that to get him to help her. So she reached out and stroked his face.

"Come on, Tommy," she said. "You wanted to help me, to save me. You can do that now."

He closed his eyes, leaned into her touch, then opened them.

"Okay."

Chapter Twenty-Five

Clint and Drake returned to Hector's place, found the man there alone, behind the bar.

"We told you to reopen," Drake said.

"I did," he said. "Nobody's come in."

"Well," Drake said, "give us two beers and tell us about Joey."

"Those fellas came back lookin' for you," Hector said, setting two beers down. "Price and the other one. Said they gave Joey your message. He's supposed to come back tonight for his gun."

"When?"

"Any time now."

"And is he bringin' his partner?"

"I dunno."

"Well," Drake said, "we're gonna sit back there. He won't see us right away when he comes in. Don't give him his gun until I tell you. Understand?"

"I understand."

"Okay," Drake said.

He and Clint walked to a table that was the furthest from the batwing doors. When Joey Getz walked in—alone or with his partner—they could be on him before he knew it.

"Okay," Clint said, "so we looked three more places for Nellie today and she wasn't there. Do you have any other suggestions?"

"She could be in somebody's barn," Drake said.

"There are a lot of barns."

"I know it."

Clint sat back in his chair and sighed.

"Don't worry," Drake said. "We're gonna find her. Or she'll find us."

"How's she going to do that?"

"We've been askin' all over for her," Drake said. "If she's hidin' out around here, she'll have heard about it."

"I hope you're right," Clint said. "I've got to get to her before whoever hired those other two sends replacements, and kills her."

"We'll find 'er," Drake said. "Maybe this Joey will tell us somethin'."

"I was stupid to let him walk out."

"Don't worry about it," Drake said. "He'll come back. He wants his gun."

"Yeah."

They drank their beers, and waited.

***

They were into a second beer, almost finished when the batwings opened, and Joey walked in. He was alone. He headed for the bar and said, "Where's my gun?"

Clint and Drake were up and behind him before he knew it.

"Not yet, Joey," Drake said.

The man turned quickly and made a face when he saw them.

"Aw shit," he said. "What now?"

"We just need to ask some questions we should've asked earlier," Clint said. "It won't take long."

"And then I get my gun?"

"And then you get it."

Joey leaned back against the bar and folded his arms.

"Okay, so ask."

"The other men said you recruited them to work for Daly and Monroe."

"That's right."

"So where did you meet those two?"

"They came into a saloon down by the water, looking for some men. Said they could pay real good. So I volunteered. They asked me if I could get three more men, so I did. That's it. Now those city dudes are dead and I don't get paid."

"What do you know about them?" Clint asked.

"Nothin'," Joey said. "Just that they said they'd pay well."

"And what made you think they could? Or would?"

"Because of the way they were dressed, and where they were stayin'. And if they didn't pay, I figured we—me and the other men—could make them once the job was done."

"So you never knew them, or saw them, before they came into that saloon?"

"No."

"Ever hear their first names?"

"No," he said. "They called each other Mister. It was very weird."

Clint looked at Drake, who shrugged.

"Yeah, okay," Clint said to Hector. "Give him his gun."

"And my partner's?" Joey asked.

"Sure."

Hector handed the man two gunbelts. Joey didn't bother to put his on right there. He just headed for the door.

"Hey!" Clint called.

"Yeah?"

"You said you figured they could pay because of where they were staying."

"That's right."

"Where was that?"

"A high falootin' hotel called The Victoria."

Clint looked at Drake.

"I know it."

"Okay," Clint said to Joey. "Go. And don't let me see you again."

"Don't worry," Joey said. "You won't."

He went out the doors.

"Let's go," Clint said. "I don't want to give him time to get brave."

"Thanks, Hector," Drake said, and they went out the doors. Joey was nowhere to be seen.

"How about the Victoria?" Clint asked.

"It's in a section of the city called Clayton," Drake said.

"What's it like there?"

"Money."

"Let's go."

"Now? It's late. I've got to eat."

"Let's eat there."

"It'll cost plenty," Drake said.

"I'll buy you dinner."

"You got a deal," Drake said. "Come on."

Chapter Twenty-Six

The Victoria hotel was on a street of high, expensive looking business buildings. Clint had seen the like in New York, but had never been to that part of St. Louis.

The hotel had five floors, and had probably been built— or finished—in the past year, it was very new looking.

"I'm not used to this part of town," Drake said, looking around. "I think St. Louis is growing too damn fast."

"The world is growing too damned fast, Drake," Clint said. "You and me, we don't belong . . . here. Especially not me. I'm a relic of the Old West."

"You're a Legend of the Old West, Clint," Drake said. "That's somethin' different. You're gonna live beyond your years. People will talk about you in a hundred years."

"I doubt it."

"Don't,"

They entered the huge hotel lobby, which had expensive furniture, marble floors, ornate lamps, and a fountain.

"Jeez," Drake said.

"Never been in here?"

"Never. And I wish I wasn't, now."

They walked to the front desk, where a well-dressed desk clerk in his forties looked them up and down. He knows, Clint thought, that we don't belong here.

"Can I help you?" he asked, doubt evident in his tone.

"Yes, we have two friends registered here: Mr. Daly and Mr. Monroe? Can you tell us what room they're in?"

"We haven't seen Mr. Daly or his friend all day."

"Is that right? But they're registered here, aren't they?" Clint asked.

"Yes, they are."

"How do you know that without lookin' it up?" Drake asked.

"Well . . . the gentlemen in question, uh, stand out. They're not like the people we usually see here."

"In what way?" Clint asked.

The man lowered his voice, ". . . they're from New York. We don't get many people here from New York."

"Well," Clint said, "we'll certainly tell them you said they were . . . odd."

The man looked shocked.

"Oh, no, no, I didn't say—I mean, I only meant—"

"I tell you what," Clint said. "Tell us what room they're in, and give us a key so we can wait for them inside, and we won't say a word."

"Really? I—well, I suppose I could—"

"Or we could talk to your manager," Drake said. "Maybe tell him what you said about your guests."

"No, no," the clerk said, "All right, I'll give you a key, but do you promise to return it?" He held it out.

Clint took it from him. "We promise. What room?"

***

They took the stairs to the third floor. Drake had headed for the elevator, but Clint admitted to him that he didn't like the things.

"Naw, me neither," Drake said.

When they got to room 303 Clint used the key to open the door, and then they hesitated.

"What if there was more than two of them?" Clint asked.

"Just what I was thinkin'," Drake said, and they both put their hands on their guns.

They went into the room fast, found nobody else in there and relaxed. Clint made sure the door was closed and locked.

"Let's take a look around," he said.

"What are we lookin' for, exactly?" Drake asked.

"I don't know," Clint said. "Something to indicate who they were taking orders from."

"You mean like this?" Drake picked something up off a writing desk that was just one of the things Clint wasn't used to seeing in hotel rooms, unless he was in New York or San Francisco.

Clint looked over and saw that Drake was holding a telegram.

"That might do it," Clint said. "What's it say?"

Drake read it aloud.

"'Orders are the same. No change.'"

"Signed by who?"

"Just the initial 'H.'"

"Where was it sent from?"

"All it says on the bottom is 'New York.'"

111

Clint took the telegram from Drake, studied it, didn't see anything else.

"Well," he said, "they were getting orders from New York, we know that much is true."

"And your girl is from New York," Drake said.

"Right."

Clint put the telegram in his pocket.

"Maybe a key operator could tell us more," he suggested. "They have to have one in a hotel like this."

"You're probably right. Let's keep looking, see if there's anything else."

But there wasn't. They searched the entire room, found clothes and personal effects, but nothing to indicate who Daly and Monroe were actually working for.

"Okay," Clint said, "let's go find the telegraph operator, and return the room key."

***

When they handed the clerk the room key back he seemed very relieved.

"Do you have a telegraph operator in the hotel?" Clint asked.

"Oh, yes sir," the clerk said. "For the convenience of our guests."

"Don't worry," Clint said, "we don't want to send anything. We just want to ask him a question."

"Well, you'll find him just at the end of that hallway." The man pointed.

"Thanks," Clint said.

As promised there was a room with a telegraph key and an operator right at the end of the hall. They showed him the telegram and asked their questions.

Yes, the telegram had come from there.

Yes, the operator had received it.

Yes, he had sent a reply.

Yes, the other end was New York City.

"Can you tell me where in New York City?"

"You mean the actual street location?" the operator said. "No, sir. There's nothing on the telegram to indicate that."

Clint handed the man a dollar.

"What's this for, sir?"

"Send a telegram and find out the location for us," Clint said, "and I'll give you another one."

"Yes, sir!"

They stood there and waited for him to send, then receive. He wrote the reply down.

"Here's the address, sir."

"And here's your other dollar."

"Thank you, sir."

As they left the room and walked back through the hall Drake asked, "Are you gonna be goin' to New York to find that telegraph key?"

"You never know," Clint said. "But first I've still got to find . . . Nellie?"

Drake thought Clint was talking to him, but then saw that he was looking past him at a young woman standing in the lobby with a boy.

"Where the hell have you been?" Clint demanded.

Chapter Twenty-Seven

They went into the hotel dining room and drew stares. None of the four of them were dressed for the place, which was on the fancy side, but they managed to get a table at the back of the room.

Clint couldn't get the boy to leave. He seemed permanently attached to Nellie Bly's side.

She introduced him as Tommy, and he introduced her to John Drake.

Then they got down to brass tacks.

"I was waiting in my hotel for you, but two men came there and I ran. I've been running and hiding ever since. Then Tommy found me on the street and hid me in his parents' barn."

"She needed help," Tommy said, pushing his jaw out pugnaciously, "and you weren't here."

"He didn't know where I was," Nellie said, in Clint's defense.

"Never mind," Clint said, "we're here now. What did the two men look like?"

"One short, one tall, wearing New York suits."

"They're dead," Drake said.

"You killed them?" Nellie asked, raising her eyebrows.

"They didn't give me a choice," Clint said.

"Who sent them?" she asked.

"We didn't have time to ask, but we just went up to their room and found this." He showed her the telegram. "You must have some idea who sent it."

"Yes, I do," she said, "but the initial isn't H."

He took the telegram back.

"Who do you think it was?"

"A man named Evander," she said, "Dr. Samuel Evander."

"Who's he?"

"He runs the asylum I went undercover in."

"And how did he find out you were there?"

"Well," she said, "he had to know, in order for me to get in. He was against it, but there was a board who approved the story. See, they thought I was going to paint a pretty picture of the place."

"And you're not?"

"Oh no," she said, "it's a horrible place and, well, I think I picked up on something they don't want exposed."

"Which is what?"

She hesitated.

"All right," he said, "we can talk about that later." He addressed both Tommy and Drake. "You fellows have been a big help, but I think we can take it from here."

"Are you leaving town?" Drake asked.

"I don't know," Clint said. "We still have a lot to talk about."

"Tommy," she said, "thanks so much. You can go home now."

116

"But . . . but . . ." the boy stammered looking at Clint, ". . . he's so old!"

"Come on, kid," Drake said, putting his hand on Tommy's shoulder, "we've been dismissed." He looked at Clint. "You know where I am."

"Thanks, John."

Tommy got to his feet reluctantly, then Drake put both hands on the boy's shoulders, turned him and marched him out.

"Who was he?" Nellie asked.

"A detective who was doing a favor helping me find you."

"Can you trust him?"

"Oh, yeah," Clint said, "he's a friend of a friend. What about the boy?"

"He doesn't know anything," she said. "He thought I was an eighteen-year-old runaway until today."

"You told him the truth?"

"Most of it."

"All right, then," he said, "we need to go somewhere else and talk. But first you need a bath and a good night's sleep."

"Where?" she asked.

"My hotel. Don't worry, you can have the bed."

They stood up and walked out. On the street she suddenly hunched her shoulders.

"Take it easy," he said. "You don't have to hide any more. The two men are dead, it's too early for any replacements to have been sent and, besides, I'm here."

She let her shoulders relax, slightly.

"Come on," he said, "we'll get you to my hotel, and tonight or tomorrow we can talk about our options."

"Our options?" she asked.

"Oh, yeah," he said. "From this point on, I'm with you."

Chapter Twenty-Eight

Clint got her to his hotel and into a hot bath. After that they sat in his room and the intention was to talk, but pretty soon her eyes started to flutter.

"Okay, off to bed with you," he said. "We can talk in the morning."

She didn't fight him. He turned down the covers and she slid into bed, wearing a long shirt she'd had in her bag. She had nothing on underneath it, and he saw a flash of hair between her legs as she got in. He had already been trying not to notice how her nipples pushed out beneath the shirt.

He covered her up so it was all out of sight.

"Where are you going to sleep?" she asked.

"There's a chair here," he said. "Don't worry about me. You need a good night's sleep."

"Yes, I do," she said, closing her eyes, "I feel safe now that you're here."

"In the morning we'll work out our plans," he told her. "All you have to do now is . . ." He stopped because she was already asleep.

He found that he was tired, as well, so he walked over to the armchair, sat, removed his boots, hung his gunbelt on the back of a wooden chair nearby, and tried to get some sleep.

***

Sometime later he opened his eyes. It was dark, with the only light a meager stream coming through the window. In that glow he saw someone approaching him, but there was no sense of danger.

"Are you asleep?" Nellie Bly whispered.

"No."

"Don't light a lamp. I—I need the dark, for what I'm going to do."

"What are you going to do?"

He felt her groping, and then she grabbed his wrists.

"This."

She tugged his wrist until his hands came in contact with her body—her bare breasts. They were like small pieces of fruit, not peaches but smaller, with hard little nipples and smooth skin.

"Nellie—"

"I'm not a virgin, if that's what you're worried about," she said. "But . . . I'm not all that experienced, either. I—I was hoping you'd come to bed, but when you didn't I knew I had to make the first move."

He took his hands away.

"Nellie, maybe you should think—"

"I've been thinking about it," she said, "ever since the day we met. But nothing happened back then. Now somebody's trying to kill me, and what if they succeed. Then this will never happen. I'd like you to lay with me tonight, just in case it's my last night."

She was being dramatic, but maybe that was because she was scared.

"Clint." She grabbed his hands again and put them back on her warm skin, which sprouted gooseflesh. "Come lay with me."

She was clearly frightened, and maybe just needed to be held. He got up from the chair and allowed himself to be led to the bed. She got in and he laid down next to her. She put her head on his shoulder and pressed her naked young body to his. He reacted as any red-blooded American man would.

She rubbed her hand over his chest, then undid a couple of buttons and slipped her hand inside his shirt. Her palm was smooth and hot on his skin. She then ran her hand down and placed it on his crotch. She could feel his hard penis through his pants, and her breath quickened audibly.

"You know I wanted you here naked, right?" she asked.

"I thought maybe—"

"You thought wrong."

Suddenly bolder, she undid his pants and slid her hand down over his belly until she was holding his cock in her hand.

"Oh, my . . ." she said, stroking it.

"Nellie," he warned, "you're asking for—"

She put her mouth to his ear. "I know what I'm asking for, Clint. Are you going to give it to me?"

He wondered if she was not as inexperienced as she would have liked him to believe?

Her hand was busy getting him harder, so he struggled out of his pants and shirt, and was finally naked next to her.

Now she ran her hand up and down the length of his penis, and underneath to cup his balls. Then her lips sought his, and he turned his head to accommodate her. She had a sweet mouth. He kissed her avidly, getting so involved in the kiss that he rolled sideways to face her. She removed her hand and his cock became trapped between them.

Not only was her mouth sweet, but the scent of her was heady. There was the slight odor of her sweat mixed with the smell of her readiness. He reached down between them to probe her, and his finger slid right into her slick pussy. She was more than ready, and so was he.

He rolled her onto her back, got between her legs, pushed the spongy head of his cock right up against her vagina while he nibbled and bit her nipples, and then lunged. She gasped, he moaned, and they fucked, pure and simple.

He couldn't tell if she was experienced or not, but she had managed to get him all worked up, and she held on for dear life—arms and legs wrapped around him—while he slammed in and out of her, making the bed shake and jump. He thought briefly about his gun, over by his chair, and knew that if anyone would burst into the room at that moment with guns blazing, he'd be dead.

But what a way to go!

Chapter Twenty-Nine

When Clint woke the next morning, Nellie was lying on his right shoulder and arm. Another bad idea. That was twice he would have been dead if someone had kicked in the door. He tried sliding out from beneath her without waking her, but it didn't work.

"W-what is it?" she asked. "What's wrong?"

"You're lying on my gun arm," he explained.

"Oh, I'm sorry," she said, her eyes widening. "Is it numb? Should I rub it?"

"No, it's fine," he said. "I just don't want to get killed after such a pleasant night."

She smiled.

"It was nice, wasn't it?" she asked. "I'm a little bruised, but I never once thought about anything except what we were doing."

"Good," Clint said, "but now we have to get back to reality. Let's get some breakfast and talk over our next move."

While they dressed she said, "I have no idea what to do when somebody's trying to kill me, except run."

"Well," Clint said, "I'm just the opposite. I believe when somebody's trying to kill you, you go on the offensive."

"So what do we do?"

"Like I said," he told her, opening the door, "we'll talk it over while we have breakfast. I'm starving!"

***

They went down to the hotel dining room and got a back table. They both ordered ham and eggs.

"Can you tell me now what you mean by take the offensive?" she asked. "You make it sound like a war."

"When somebody's trying to kill you, it is a war," he said. "Whoever sent those two—this mysterious 'H'—is going to send somebody else."

"So what do we do?"

"We arrange for you not to be here."

"Where will I be?"

"Back in New York."

"But . . . that's where all this started. That's where they came from."

"That's going on the offensive," he said. "You go where they don't expect you to go."

"What am I supposed to do in New York?"

"Whatever I tell you to do."

"You're going to be with me?"

"Right by your side, until this is all over."

"Well," she said, "that doesn't sound so bad, then. Do I let my editor know I'm coming?"

"Not a word to anyone," he said. "We're going to slip into Manhattan with no one the wiser."

"Then what?"

"Then we find out who this mysterious 'H' is, and what the hell is going on."

"She was quiet.

"Or do you already know?"

"I have suspicions."

"Do you want to tell me about them?"

"Well . . . while I was in there, I heard some things, some conversations . . . oh hell, I think that Doctor Evander is using his patients as . . . assassins for hire."

"What?"

"I heard him talking to someone on the telephone—the asylum has two—and he was accepting a job to have someone killed. He said he had just the homicidal maniac in a cell who could do the job."

"Who was he talking to?"

"I don't know," she said. "I couldn't hear the other side of the conversation."

"Who was going to be killed?"

"A politician named Colton."

"And has he been killed since you heard this?"

"I don't know," she said. "I haven't seen a newspaper recently."

"Well, we can find out," he said. "How long ago was this?"

"I've lost track of time," she said. "Weeks?"

"Could he have been talking to this 'H'?"

"I guess so."

It hadn't really been a question. He was just wondering out loud.

"So when do we go back?" she asked.

"As soon as I get tickets."

"What about your horse?" she asked. "That great big, beautiful horse?"

"I left him in Texas," Clint said. "I took the train to get here to you as fast as I could."

She put her fork down and stared down at her plate.

"I'm really sorry I sent you that telegram, but you're the only one I could think of," she said. "And you did tell me back in Denver that if I was ever in trouble—"

"Relax, Nellie," he said, cutting her off. "I'm happy to come and help you."

"Also . . . I'm just about broke," she said.

"I'll buy the tickets back to New York," he said, "and pay the expenses while we're there."

"As soon as we get this all straightened out," she said, "and I write my story, I know I can get my editor to reimburse you."

"That's fine," he said. "I'll keep track of expenses if that'll make you feel better."

"Thank you," she said. "It will."

"Are you finished here?" he asked. "We might as well get to the railroad station and see about those tickets. I'm sure we can get on a train today.

"That'd be great."

"Then you can tell me everything you went through while you were on the run."

"And you can tell me what you did while you were look-ing for me."

He stood up. "Clearly we still have a lot to talk about."

Chapter Thirty

Manhattan, New York City

Clint knew a private detective who lived in Brooklyn named Delvecchio, who had helped him once before. He sent the man a telegram before they got on the train, but had to leave before a reply came back.

As they got off the train in Manhattan he told Nellie, "If Delvecchio got my telegram he'll be here, or he'll send somebody."

"How many times have you been East?" she asked.

"I've been to New York many times, but I was also born in the East."

"Really? The Gunsmith, a legend of the Old West, was born here?" she asked.

"Not in New York, but—wait a minute." He stopped short. "This isn't an interview."

"Sorry," she said, "I was just making conversation."

"I wonder why all your attempts at making conversation come in the form of a question?" he asked.

There were a lot of people on the platform, going to and from trains. Clint's Colt was in his carpetbag—one of two hurriedly purchased in St. Louis—but his .25 Colt New Line was in his belt, tucked in the small of his back, where no New York policeman could see it. He was not up to date on the New York laws concerning carrying guns on the street.

"I'd like to go home and pick up some things—" she started, but he cut her off.

"Not a chance," he said. "That's the one place they'll be looking for you. We have to go someplace else."

"Can't we go to one of the hotels where you usually stay?" Nellie asked.

"No," he said, "they're too high profile. We need a hotel that's out of the way, but not a flea trap."

Clint noticed a man approaching him from out of the crowd, a telegram in his hand.

"Don't say anything," he told Nellie. "Let me do the talking."

The man might have been a lawman, but as he reached them he handed Clint the telegram. It was the one he had sent Delvecchio."

"Del couldn't make it," he said, "but he sent me."

"Where is he?"

"In the hospital," the man said.

"Bad?"

"He'll be okay, but out of commission for a while."

"That's too bad," Clint said. "I'm sure his wife will be upset."

"She would," the man said, "if he had one. He ain't married."

"He could've sent his brother in his place."

"He could've," the man said, "if he had one. Any more tests?"

Clint stuck his hand out. "Clint Adams."

"My name's Jacoby," the man said, pronouncing it Jack-o-bee. "You can call me Jack."

"Are you also a private detective?"

"Yeah, only while Del lives in Brooklyn, I live here, in Manhattan. He thought I might be useful."

"I hope he's right."

Jacoby looked at Nellie, who as per instructions had not said a word.

"Is this the problem?" Jacoby asked.

"Yes. We need a place to stay, out of the way, but not rundown."

"I've got just the place for ya," Jacoby said. "Ma'am, can I carry your carpetbag?"

She looked at Clint, who nodded.

"Thank you," she said, handing it over.

"This way. I've got a hansom cab out front so you won't be traveling out in the open."

"Good thinking," Clint said.

"Well, when Del told me who you are, I figured you wouldn't want to be shot at on the street."

They walked through the train station to the street, where the cab was waiting.

"No driver?" Clint asked.

"I'll drive," Jacoby said. "I figured the less people involved, the better."

"Also good thinking," Clint said. "Thanks."

He and Nellie got in the back. Jacoby climbed up top and got underway.

"Can we trust him?" Nellie whispered.

129

"If we trust that Delvecchio sent him, then we can trust him," Clint said.

"And you're sure?"

"Not yet."

***

They drove for awhile, and then Clint felt the cab stop. When the door opened he had his hand on his gun, but it was Jacoby and he was alone.

"We're here."

Clint got out, Jacoby helped Nellie down. People were walking the streets, but not paying any special attention to them.

"Where are we?" Clint asked.

"Little Italy," Jacoby said, "just across from Chinatown. People tend to mind their own business, here."

"Which building?" Clint asked.

"This one," Jacoby said, indicating the three-story brick structure they had stopped in front of.

"Is this a hotel?" Nellie asked.

"Better," Jacoby said, grabbing her carpetbag. "It's a safe house. Come on."

"A safe house?" she asked.

"Someplace we put people—witnesses, victims—to keep them safe."

"We?" Clint asked.

"Yeah," Jacoby said, "I used to be a policeman."

"What happened?"

"Too many rules."

"So was this used by the police?"

"No," Jacoby said. "This is mine."

He used a key to unlock the front door and they went inside. Clint and Nellie followed him up a flight of stairs, came to a door where he used another key. The interior was dark as they stopped just inside the doorway.

"Hold on," he said, and went off into the dark. He lit a lamp, then another, and still another, and they were finally able to see the expanse of the floor. The ceiling was high, there was a kitchen setup off to one side, a sofa and chairs in the center, and a big bed off to another side.

"Eighteen hundred square feet," Jacoby said, "and the windows are blacked out so nobody can see the light. Nobody's gonna take a shot at you while you're here."

"This is fine," Clint said.

"I can bring some food up for you, if you like," Jacoby said. "Some stuff you can cook on that stove, which works, by the way."

"That sounds good, too," Clint said. "Thanks, Jack."

"I don't know exactly what you're here for," Jacoby said, "but let me know how I can help, and I will."

"You've already helped a lot," Clint said, "but I do have one question."

"What's that?"

"Do you know a politician named Colton?"

"I do, yeah," Jacoby said. "He was all set to run for Mayor."

"Was?" Nellie asked.

"Yeah," Jacoby said. "Assemblyman Frank Colton was assassinated a week ago."

Chapter Thirty-One

Jacoby explained that Colton was strangled to death in his home. His wife found him the next morning.

"At first they said it was a break-in," he went on, "but then everyone—the police, politicians, newspapers—all decided that he was assassinated."

Clint and Nellie exchanged a glance.

"You know somethin' about that?"

"We might," Clint said.

"So that's why you're here?"

"Partially."

When they said nothing further Jacoby said, "Well, let me go and get some food, and while I'm gone you can decide just how much you want to tell me."

"We appreciate it," Clint said.

"I'll bring some whiskey, too," Jacoby added, "just in case somebody needs a stiff drink."

"Sounds good," Clint said.

They waited until they heard the downstairs door slam closed before speaking.

"Are we going to trust him?"

"If he comes back alone with food and whiskey," Clint said, "I'd say yes."

"And why would you say no?"

"If he comes back with somebody who tries to kill us."

***

But when Jacoby returned it was only with a carton of food and a bottle of whiskey. They stored the food in cupboards, then cracked the seal on the whiskey and each had a drink.

With Nellie's permission, Clint told Jacoby about her asylum story, and what she discovered while behind those walls.

"The Woman's Lunatic Asylum on Blackwell Island?"

"That's the one," Nellie said.

"Where is that, exactly?" Clint asked.

"It's in the East River," Nellie said. "You have to take a boat to get there, either from this side, or Brooklyn."

"This is quite a story," Jacoby said. "That asylum gets support from the city. If this gets out, it could blow the lid off New York politics."

"I thought I was writing an exposé," Nellie said. "I thought I'd just write it and that would be the end of it, but that was before somebody tried to kill me."

"Wait," Jacoby asked, "was there an actual attempt on you?"

"I didn't wait for that," Nellie said. "I was being followed, and then someone broke into my home. I got out of New York before they could find me."

"So then nobody actually tried to kill you?" Jacoby persisted.

"I didn't give them that chance," she explained.

"She was followed to St. Louis, where two men tried to catch her in her hotel," Clint said.

"And what happened to them?"

"I had to kill them before finding out who they worked for. But we found this in their hotel room."

He handed Jacoby the telegram he'd found.

"Do you have any idea who this mysterious 'H,'" might be?" Clint asked.

"There are a couple of 'H's' in New York politics," Jacoby said. "Herman MacDonald runs the carters, or teamsters, down on the docks. Every shipment that comes into New York gets unloaded by them."

"And the other?"

"There's an Assemblyman named Richard R. Head," Jacoby said. "Everybody in New York calls him 'Dick' Head."

"And why would one of them be involved with an assassination squad made up of lunatics?" Clint asked.

"Well," Jacoby said, "for one thing it's probably profitable, and on the other hand, politicians often need somebody killed in order to get their way."

"What's your guess?" Clint asked. "Which one sent that telegram?"

"I don't know," Jacoby said. "They're both scum."

"So how do we find out?" Nellie asked.

"Oh, that's simple," Clint said.

"It is?" Jacoby asked.

"Sure," Clint said. "I'm just going to ask them."

Chapter Thirty-Two

Jacoby left, promising to return the next day, if that's what they wanted.

"We can use all the help we can get," Clint said. "By the way, what hospital is Delvecchio in?"

"Brooklyn Hospital."

"That sounds very fitting," Clint said, "considering how much he loves Brooklyn. Look, give him my best and tell him I'll try to stop in and see him before I leave New York."

"You got it," Jacoby said.

After Jacoby left, Clint and Nellie looked over the food, and she said she could make a stew, if he was willing to risk her cooking.

"Go ahead," he told her. "It's got to be better than mine. I can cook over a campfire, but that's about it."

While she prepared the meal, Clint walked around the eighteen hundred square foot space, to see what they were working with. They had a bathtub and sink in a corner, with running water. There was one bed, but the sofa looked capable to being slept on. He wasn't sure what they were going to do about that one night they'd had in St. Louis. Clint didn't want Nellie Bly to form too much of an attachment to him, and by the same token he didn't want to become too fond of her. They should stay friends, and if that was going to happen, then she should take the bed, and he the couch.

"Supper's ready," she called out.

"It smells great!"

They sat at the table and ate, washing it down with small glasses of whiskey, and large glasses of water.

"What's our first move tomorrow morning?" she asked.

"Your first and only move is staying here," he told her. "You're safe here. As for me, I'm going to see if I can talk to those two 'H's,' and maybe even visit the asylum and talk to Doctor Evander."

"You better be careful," she said. "If they locked you in there, it would be next to impossible to get out."

"How did you get out?"

"I had a contact," she said. "Her name is Nurse Carol—Carol Whitney. When I was ready to give up my phony identity, she got me out."

"Then I better talk to her, too,"

"You'll like her," Nellie said. "She's older than I am and even though we didn't have that much in common, I believe we became friends."

"That's good, but tell me . . . if they want you dead, why didn't they just kill you while you were in there, and make it seem like an accident?"

"I don't think they decided they wanted me dead until I was out," she said. "I'm afraid I talked to too many people about the story I wanted to write."

"So you don't know which friends told the asylum people?" he asked.

"No."

"I'll need the names of the people who knew."

"I'll write them down, but you won't be able to talk to all of them in one day."

"No problem," he said. "I'll do it in two."

"What about the police?" she asked. "The New York police are notoriously crooked."

"If that's the case, and we can't trust them, we'll have to trust Jack to help us, and that's it," he said. "When I know who's behind the threats on your life, I'll take care of them and then you can do what you want. Talk to the police, write about it, whatever."

"And what will you do?"

"Get out of town," he said. "Fast!"

"And I won't mention you to anyone," she said. "That's brilliant. If no one knows you're here, no one can accuse you of anything."

"That's right," he said, "but I don't know if I can go completely unnoticed. Not if I'm going to talk to people. I just won't be talking to the police."

"You've been to New York before."

"Many times."

"Don't you know any honest policeman?"

"Every time I come to town, the policemen I knew are gone, replaced by new ones," he said, with a shrug. "That's just the way it is."

When they finished eating she cleaned up the plates and utensils, and then made coffee. Once again, they sat at the table.

"So I just stay here until it's all over?" she asked.

"That's right."

She looked around.

"It's not as bad as what you were dealing with in St. Louis," he said. "And I'll be able to move around more easily knowing that you're safe and sound, here."

"Yes," she said, "all right. I suppose I could use the time to write."

"Great idea," he said. "Write your story."

"While you work on the ending."

"Right."

She thought about it for a moment, then said, "Yeah, okay, I can do that."

"Good."

After coffee she cleaned the cups in the sink, which also had running water. Then she turned to face him, drying her hands.

"We can share the bed," she said.

"That's probably not a good idea, Nellie," he said. "We need to keep this . . . friendly. Not get too involved. We can't let our feelings take over."

"Yes, of course," she said. "All right, I agree."

"So you take the bed, and I'll take the sofa," he said. "And let's turn in early and get a good night's sleep."

"Agreed," she said. "I'll go and change for bed first."

He nodded. She grabbed her bag and took it into the water closet with her, closing the door firmly behind her.

Chapter Thirty-Three

It was awkward, sleeping on the couch when Nellie was sleeping in bed, only about ten feet away, but they made it work. They stayed where they were until morning, and then she got up and made breakfast.

Jacoby had brought eggs, bacon and the makings for biscuits.

"You're a good cook," Clint said, while they ate.

"I learned at an early age."

"Are you as good a writer as you are a cook?"

She smiled. "Better."

There was a knock on the upstairs door while they were still eating. They had agreed that Jacoby could use his key for the downstairs, but that he would knock before coming in upstairs.

"Come in!" Clint yelled.

Jacoby entered. Calling out, "Good morning."

"Sit down," Nellie said. "I made breakfast."

"Oh, good," Jacoby said. "I haven't eaten."

He sat down and she put a cup of coffee and a plate of bacon-and-eggs in front of him. Then she sat and pushed the basket of biscuits toward him.

"This is good," he said.

"Thanks."

He looked at Clint.

"Have you made any plans?"

"Nellie will be staying up here," Clint said. "I'm going out today and talk to people."

"Who?"

"The two you told me about, the teamster and assembly-man who are 'H's.' Then the doctor at the asylum and a nurse who Nellie said she worked with named Whitney, Carol Whitney."

"What doctor?"

"His name's Evander," Nellie said. "He runs the asy-lum."

"You're gonna need back-up," Jacoby said to Clint. "If you'll let me, I'll come along with you, make sure you don't get shot in the back."

"You think somebody would do that?" Nellie asked.

"If they were gonna kill you, they wouldn't think twice about killin' Clint," Jacoby said, looking at her and then back to Clint. "Will you let me?"

"Do you have a gun?" Clint asked.

"I do."

"Can you use it?"

"I'm not a Legend of the West like you are, but yeah, I can use it."

"Okay then," Clint said. "I'd appreciate the back-up."

"Good," Jacoby said. "I wouldn't want to have to explain to Delvecchio that I let his friend get killed."

"Did you see him last night, or this morning?" Clint asked.

"Last night," Jacoby said. "When I told him what was going on he almost got out of bed to come here. A doctor and I talked him out of it."

"He's a good friend."

"And you don't want to see him get killed, either," Jacoby said. "If he tried to help in the condition he's in, that's what would happen."

"I'm glad you got him to stay put, then."

Jacoby wolfed down the breakfast, then they all had another cup of coffee before Clint and he got up to leave.

"What are the gun laws in New York right now?" Clint asked.

"There's a law against minorities carrying guns," Jacoby said. "It's leftover from the Civil War, when black slaves weren't allowed to carry. Here they don't want Chinese, Irish, German and other minorities to carry."

"Okay, then" Clint said. "I'll wear my gun. And I'll leave one for Nellie."

"A gun? For me?" Nellie asked. "I've never fired a gun."

"It's just in case somebody comes by while we're not here," Clint explained.

"But nobody knows I'm here."

"I'm just playing it safe." He got the .25 Colt New Line from his bag and took it over to her. Very quickly, he gave her a lesson on firing a gun.

"Point," he said, "and shoot. That's it."

She held the gun like it was a dead rat.

"I don't know if I'll be able to do it," she said.

"If someone is here to kill you," Jacoby told her, "trust me, you'll do it."

***

Down on the street Jacoby showed Clint to a buggy he had brought with him.

"I thought it would be better for me to drive, rather than use a driver we might not be able to trust."

"Good thinking," Clint said.

"Where do you want to go first?" Jacoby asked.

"Let's make it the asylum," Clint said. "How do we get out there?"

"We'll have to take a boat."

"Do you know anybody who might be able to get us in?" Clint asked.

"Well," Jacoby said, "I know some doctors. But we won't be able to go out there today. I'll have to talk to them, first"

"Okay, then how about the politician?" Clint asked. And the teamster?"

"Herman MacDonald has an office on the East River docks," Jacoby said. "He'll be the easiest to get to."

"And the other one? Head?"

"He has an office downtown," Jacoby said. "We can go and catch him there after MacDonald."

"Okay, Jack," Clint said. "I'm in your hands."

"Then the docks it is," Jacoby said.

Chapter Thirty-Four

Jacoby took Clint to a set of docks at the mouth of the Hudson River where it met New York Harbor. Out in the middle of the harbor stood the recently dedicated Statue of Liberty, which had been a gift to America from France.

"You know," Clint said, "I almost came to New York for the dedication ceremonies of that statue."

"What changed your mind?"

"I had a bad experience at another dedication ceremony."

"Well, you're lucky you didn't come. It was a mad-house."

Jacoby pulled his buggy to the side and stopped.

"So where's MacDonald?" Clint asked.

"He has an office in the Warehouse 13 building, over there." Jacoby pointed.

"Do you know him?"

"I do, yeah."

"Then you can get us in."

"Well," Jacoby said, "that could be a problem. See, he and I don't get along. In fact, he hates me."

"So you don't want to go in?"

"No, just the opposite," Jacoby said. "I do, but I want you to understand what's happening."

"Okay. So how do we do this?"

"Like you said," Jacoby answered, "the simple way is the best. If we just want to ask him, then we should just simply walk in."

"Great," Clint said. "Lead the way."

They walked along the docks, where men were loading and unloading ships that had arrived or were departing soon. No one paid them much attention, until they actually approached the warehouse.

"Uh-oh," Jacoby said.

"What?"

"I thought we'd have to talk our way in," he said, "but see that man coming out? That's MacDonald."

Clint saw a rough-hewn, stocky man who had probably come up from the docks himself, to the position he now held. He was wearing a suit, but he had no jacket on, and his shirt sleeves were rolled up to expose thick forearms. He had three men hanging on every word he was saying.

As they approached the warehouse he spotted them, and obviously recognize Jacoby.

"What the hell do you want?" MacDonald demanded.

"Nice to see you, too, Herman," the detective said. "But actually, it's not me who wants to see you, but my friend, here. He has some questions."

"Well," MacDonald said, "I don't have any interest in any friend of yours, Jacoby, so take a walk—preferably off a short pier."

"Very clever," Jacoby said, "but my friend won't take no for an answer."

MacDonald studied Clint for a moment, saw that beneath the jacket he was wearing a gunbelt.

"This ain't the Wild West, ya know?" MacDonald said. "You ain't gonna intimidate me with a gun."

"My friend's name is Clint Adams, Herman," Jacoby said. "I think you better give him a few minutes."

MacDonald studied Clint again, this time more intently

"You got quite a reputation, Adams," MacDonald said. "In fact, I even hear you got some accomplishments hereabouts, as well as in the West."

"I get around," Clint said.

"I guess you do," MacDonald said. "All right, I'll see you in my office." He looked at Jacoby and pointed. "Not you!"

"No problem," Jacoby said. "I'll wait out here."

"Follow me, Adams."

"You want us to come up with you, Boss?" one of the longshoremen asked.

"No," MacDonald said. "I'm fine, but why don't you three keep Jacoby company."

"Sure, Boss." All three men glared at the detective.

"This way, Adams."

He led Clint into the warehouse, across the floor to a metal stairway that led up to an office. When they reached it MacDonald opened the door and said, "After you."

Clint entered, MacDonald followed and shut the door. The walls were mostly glass, supposedly so MacDonald could see out in all directions and at all times.

MacDonald walked to a desk and stood behind it. He did not sit.

"I ain't gonna offer you a drink, because I gotta feelin' this ain't exactly a social call."

"You're right," Clint said. "I have a friend that somebody is trying to kill."

"And you're comin' to me about this . . . why?"

"The person who's trying to have her killed has the initial 'H,'" Clint explained.

"First or last initial?" MacDonald asked.

"I don't know."

"And who else are you gonna talk to besides me?"

"A politician named Head."

MacDonald laughed. "'Dick Head? You suspect him of tryin' to have somebody killed?"

"Him, or you."

"And who's the prospective victim?"

Clint was impressed that MacDonald could go from street talk to something a little more progressive, like the word "prospective." He thought the man might be a little more educated than he wanted people to know.

"A journalist."

"Ah, well, there you go," MacDonald said. "There are any number of people in this town who might want to kill a journalist."

"You included?"

"Probably," MacDonald said, "depending on who we're talkin' about."

"For now, I'm not ready to say."

"Then I can't help you," MacDonald said. "If I don't know the name, I don't know if I want them killed, do I?"

Chapter Thirty-Five

"I tell you what," MacDonald said. "When you decide you wanna tell me the name of this journalist, I'll be happy to tell you if I wish they were dead. But I don't think I'm gonna be killin' anybody in the near future."

"Or having them killed?"

"Or having them killed," MacDonald agreed. "Now, you want a glass of Irish Whiskey before you go?"

"Sure, why not?"

***

MacDonald walked Clint back outside after they'd had a glass of Irish together.

"How'd you get mixed up with Jacoby?" MacDonald asked, as they walked back across the warehouse floor.

"He's the friend of a friend."

"So you don't know him?"

"Just met him yesterday."

"Well," MacDonald said, "you only met me today, but I'd warn you against trustin' him."

"Why's that?"

"Ask him," MacDonald said. "Ask him why I hate him and don't trust him. See what he says."

As they came out onto the dock they saw Jacoby and the three longshoremen, all smoking and waiting. MacDonald's men had formed a semi-circle around the detective.

"That it?" Jacoby asked, discarding his cigarette. "All done?"

"For now," Clint said. He looked at MacDonald. "Thanks for the drink."

"Don't mention it."

For a moment Clint thought MacDonald was going to offer his hand, and he didn't know if he'd shake it or not. It would have been the Irishman's way of digging at Jacoby, making him think that he and Clint had formed a bond of some sort. But in the end, he wasn't faced with that decision. MacDonald kept his hands at his sides.

"Let's go, then," Jacoby said. "I need some fresh air."

They started walking back to their buggy.

"How did that go?" Jacoby asked.

"I'm not sure," Clint said. "He sounded convincing. If he tried to have anybody killed lately he's certainly unconcerned about it."

"That's because he has most of the New York Police Department in his pocket," Jacoby said.

"Is it as corrupt as I've heard?" Clint asked.

"Worse. It was supposed to be real bad just after the Civil War, but from what I've heard it's even worse now."

"That's a shame," Clint said.

"So I guess you'll just have to stick with trusting me," Jacoby said, as they reached the buggy.

Clint turned, saw Herman MacDonald still standing there watching them. He decided not to ask Jacoby the question MacDonald had suggested he ask.

Not yet, anyway.

***

Assemblyman Richard R. Head, had an office in the City Hall area of downtown Manhattan.

"You usually can't get in to see a politician without an appointment," Jacoby said.

"But you happen to know this one?"

"Never met him," Jacoby admitted. "All I know is what I've read."

"So how do you intend to get us in?"

"I know some of the guards in the building," Jacoby said. "If one of them is on duty we might get in."

"And if not?"

Jacoby looked at him.

"You just might have to make an appointment."

***

"What about your own New York connections?" Jacoby asked, as they reached downtown.

Clint told Jacoby the same thing he had told Nellie.

"Every time I come here, all my connections have moved on," he explained. "Except for Delvecchio, that is."

"And now me," Jacoby said. "This is my home and I ain't leavin'."

"Are you an ex-policeman?" Clint asked.

"Nope," Jacoby said, "ex-boxer."

"You couldn't tell that from your face," Clint said.

"I know," Jacoby said. "I was fast, hard to hit."

"And what happened?"

"I was too light," he said, "and one day this big guy managed to hit me."

"And?"

"Knocked me into the middle of next week," Jacoby said. "I gave it up, then. I hit the streets, tried learning all I could."

"And became a detective."

"I'm not really licensed," Jacoby said. "I sort of freelance, do a lot of work for lawyers and other detectives, like Del. But I've learned the trade."

"Then why not get a license?"

"I'd be limited in what I could do," Jacoby explained. "And the crooked police could always threaten my license. This way, I can't be threatened with anything."

"Good point."

Jacoby stopped the buggy underneath a stone arch and said, "We'll have to walk from here. We don't want to be seen comin'."

They got out and started walking.

"His office is in a building on Park Row, about a block from City Hall."

"What do you know about this man?"

151

"That he's ambitious," Jacoby said. "Supposedly the view from his window is actually of City Hall, where he hopes to one day be Mayor."

"That sounds like something worth killing for."

"It sure does."

Chapter Thirty-Six

When they got to the building they wanted, Jacoby said, "Why don't you wait out here? Lemme see who's on duty in the lobby."

"Okay."

Clint stood out on the paved sidewalk, looking the street over while Jacoby went inside. There were people hustling their way to and from work, and none of them were paying him any mind. A policeman walked by, looked him up and down, but decided not to approach him and moved on.

"Clint!"

He turned, saw Jacoby half in and half out the doorway.

"Yeah?"

"Come on," Jacoby said. "A friend of mine is gettin' us in."

"For free?"

"No. You got two dollars?"

"I've got two dollars."

Clint handed the money over, and they went inside. There was a curved front desk with a uniformed guard seated behind it. Jacoby hurried over to the desk, surreptitiously passed the man the two dollars, and then led the way to the elevator.

"Is this necessary?" Clint asked.

"It's on the fourth floor."

Clint hesitated.

"You don't like elevators?"

"I don't like elevators."

"Well, there's a stairway," Jacoby said, "right over there, but I'm taking the elevator."

"Yeah, okay."

Jacoby thought "Yeah okay," meant that Clint would take the elevator with him, but when the doors closed they did so with him inside the elevator, and Clint on the outside.

When he got to the fourth floor he only had to wait a few moments, for Clint to come out of the stairwell, slightly out of breath.

"What room?" Clint asked.

"Four-oh-two."

They walked past 400 and 401 than stopped in front of 402, which had ASSEMBLYMAN RICHARD R. HEAD written on it. Jacoby opened the door without knocking.

A girl looked up from her desk and smiled at them, then gave a little frown.

"Yes?"

"Is the Assemblyman in?" Clint asked.

"Who's calling?" she asked.

"My name is Clint Adams."

The frown deepened.

"Do you have an appointment?"

"No," Clint said, and then something occurred to him. "But tell him it's about the Woman's Lunatic Asylum on Blackwell Island."

That seemed to frighten her a bit. She stood and said, "Wait here, please," then opened the door behind her desk and entered Head's office.

"Was that wise?" Jacoby asked.

"If he agrees to see us," Clint said, "then the asylum means something to him."

"Good point."

When she opened the door, and stepped out she said, "You can go in now, gentlemen."

"Thank you," Clint said.

He went first, followed by Jacoby, who seemed willing to let Clint take the lead, here.

Assemblyman Head was standing behind a large, oak desk. Behind him was a large window with a panoramic view of downtown Manhattan, including City Hall. He was a tall, slender man in his forties, and had a politician's smile plastered on his face—the kind that has no relation, whatsoever, to the eyes.

"Gentlemen," Head said, "which of you is Mr. . . . Adams, was it?"

"That's right," Clint said. "Clint Adams."

"And you are?" Head asked, looking at Jacoby.

"I'm just watchin'," Jacoby said.

"I see." Head turned his attention to Clint. "What can I do for you? Mary said something about an . . . asylum?"

"Yes," Clint said, "the Woman's Asylum on Blackwell Island."

Head shook his head. "Is that supposed to mean something to me?"

"Only if they're using their inmates as paid assassins and you know about it," Clint said.

"I—what? I don't understand? I'm supposed to know about this place?"

"If you didn't know about it," Clint said, "you wouldn't have agreed to see us."

"And in hindsight, that may have been a mistake."

"Well, it's too late now, Dick," Jacoby said, "so why don't you sit down and listen?"

"I beg your pardon?"

Clint swept his jacket aside so the man could see the gun in his holster.

"Sit!" he said.

"Oh, my," Head said, and sat heavily.

"Nice view, Mr. Head," Clint said. "Hoping to make it to City Hall someday?"

"It's a possibility."

"Willing to murder for that chance?" Clint asked.

"Look, you're not making any sense," Head complained. "Who am I supposed to have murdered? And what's this about assassins in the asylum? This is all very strange."

"I don't think so," Clint said. He took out the telegram signed by "H" and tossed it on the desk. "I think you sent that."

Head eyed Clint and Jacoby carefully as he reached for the telegram. He read it briefly, then dropped it like it was hot.

"I think you should leave," he said. "In fact, how did you even get into the building?"

"Mr. Head," Clint began, "I have a friend who's a journalist. If any harm comes to her, I'm coming for you."

"I—wha—you're crazy."

"Those two men, Daly and his partner, didn't get the job done in St. Louis," Clint said. "In case you were wondering, I killed them."

Clint had learned to read faces over the years. Richard Head looked as if he had just learned the answer to something he was wondering about.

"That's right," Clint said, "she's still alive, and she's getting ready to write her story."

"Look," Head said, "I don't know what you're talking about. Now I think you better leave."

Clint looked at Jacoby, who nodded. He was reading the man, as well.

"Just remember what I said," Clint told him.

Head was slumped in his chair, scowling furiously as Clint and Jacoby left the office.

***

Down on the street Clint said, "You get the same read I did?"

"Yeah," Jacoby said. "He's your 'H,' all right. He like swallowed his tongue when you told him you killed his men in St. Louis and Miss Bly was still alive."

"I don't think I ever told you her name," Clint said.

"You didn't have to," Jacoby said. "I read *The New York World*. And I've seen her around. She's Nellie Bly, all right."

157

Clint studied Jacoby.

"Okay, don't start suspectin' me," Jacoby said. "I'm on your side, remember?"

"I remember," Clint said. If Jacoby was working with Head, Clint figured he would have been dead by now—or Nellie would have. No, Jacoby was right, he couldn't start suspecting the detective at this stage of the game.

"Okay, what about those doctors you know?" Clint asked.

"I've still got time today," Jacoby said. "Why don't you go back to Nellie, and I'll come by later and tell you what I find out."

"You've got a deal."

***

Richard Head waited until he was sure the two men were gone, then went out and said to his secretary, "I need Bennett Wilkes."

"I'll have to find him—"

"Well, do it!" Head said. "I need him here in the next hour!"

He went back into his office and slammed the door.

Wilkes was his problem guy. If he had a problem, it was Bennett Wilkes who found the men to take care of it. If the Gunsmith—and Head had certainly recognized the man's name—was right, then Wilkes had gotten those men from the Woman's Lunatic Asylum. Head wanted to hear it right from Wilkes' own lips. If it was true, and Nellie Bly was going to write about it, she needed to be taken care of as soon as possible.

Chapter Thirty-Seven

"I've been wondering when you'd get back!" Nellie blurted as Clint entered. "Where's Jack?"

"He's checking on getting us into the asylum to see Dr. Evander."

"Did you find out anything?"

Clint sniffed the air. "How about a cup of coffee first?"

"Oh, of course," she said. "Sorry."

She poured him a cup and they sat at the table together.

"Anything?"

"I think we found your Mr. 'H,'" he told her.

"Who is it?"

"Richard Head."

"That figures," she said. "The politician. Is he going to use assassins to get himself into the Mayor's mansion?"

"Seems like that's the plan," Clint said. "His office has quite a view of City Hall."

"How did you find out?"

"Jack and I visited him, told him about his men being killed in St. Louis, and showed him the telegram he sent them."

"And he admitted it?"

"No," Clint said, "but his face did."

"So you're saying you read it on his face that he's the guy," she said.

"Jacoby read it, too. We agreed on it."

"Did you see the other one?"

"MacDonald? Yeah," Clint said. "He seems like a pretty straightforward guy. I think if he wanted to kill you he'd walk up to you and do it."

"So what's next?"

"Like I said, I want to get into that asylum to see the doctor. Maybe we can get him to turn on Head."

"And what if he's the man in charge?" she asked.

"Then maybe we can get Head to turn on him," Clint said.

"And if neither of them will turn?"

"Then we just need to get enough information for you to write your story," Clint said. "If we get into the asylum, I want to see that nurse you mentioned, too . . . Whitney?"

"Carol Whitney."

"Right, her," Clint said. "If she talked to you, she might talk to me, and maybe she'll turn on both of them. There's always a weak link. We just have to find it."

"So what are we doing right now?"

"Now we're waiting for Jack," Clint said. "He'll be by later."

"Well," she said, "I have enough here to make supper, so I'll have it ready when he gets here."

"Good idea."

"And you can help," she said.

"What do you want me to do?"

"I want the Gunsmith to cut some vegetables."

Chapter Thirty-Eight

Bennett Wilkes entered Richard Head's office and said, "You wanted to see me?"

"Damn right I wanted to see you!" Head said. "What the hell is this about the Woman's Lunatic Asylum using their patients as paid assassins?"

Wilkes didn't make any attempt to deny it.

"Where'd you hear about that?"

"A man by the name of Clint Adams was in here today, throwing it in my face. Are we involved with this?"

"Well," Wilkes said, "when you need somethin' done, and you tell me you don't care how I do it, yeah, I use them."

"Who the hell is in charge over there?"

"His name's Dr. Evander," Wilkes said. "He's found himself a nice little sideline to make money."

"Murder?"

Wilkes shrugged. "That's what some people would call it."

"So when we sent Daly and Monroe to St. Louis to take care of this Bly character, they came from the asylum?"

"Well, no," Wilkes said, "that time I picked out the men. Why? What happened to them?"

"The Gunsmith killed them!"

"Oh."

"And now he's in town trying to find out who sent them, and he's decided it was me."

"Well, it was, sort of . . ."

"Did you send a telegram to St. Louis and sign it with my initial?"

"I had to tell Daly and Monroe they were workin' for you."

"Why?"

"They wouldn't have gone, otherwise," Wilkes said. "They both said they'd vote for you if you ever ran for Mayor. That they'd do anythin' they could to help."

"So to get their votes, we sent them to murder somebody."

"In a way, yes," Wilkes said. "Look, this Bly girl was gonna write about conditions at the asylum. Then she heard Evander talkin' on the phone with me, and he mentioned your name."

"For godssake, why?"

"Well, he also said he'd vote for you."

"Jesus . . ." Head said, almost under his breath, "so I'm not involved with this assassin business, but it could all come tumbling down on me if she writes about it."

"Well, yeah," Wilkes said. "I mean . . . you wanted her dead, right?"

"Because she's an up-and-comer," Head said, "she's a journalist who could hurt me in the press if she ever decided to write about me."

"So you wanted her killed just in case?"

"I didn't even want her killed, Wilkes," Head said, "I wanted her scared."

"You told me to handle her."

"Right," Head said, "I didn't tell you to kill her."

"Well, 'handle' means 'kill,'" Wilkes said. "And Dr. Evander wanted her killed, too."

"But you don't work for Dr. Evander, you work for me."

"Let's just say I found a little sideline of my own."

"So you're involved in the whole assassin thing?"

"Evander had the personnel, but not the contacts, so . . ." He shrugged.

"So because you wanted a sideline, I'm involved."

"Yeah," Wilkes said, "sorry about that."

Head sat back in his chair and put his hands over his face. Wilkes had managed to put his entire political future in jeopardy. This whole situation had gotten out of hand, thanks to idiot Bennett Wilkes.

"Okay, Bennett?" he said. "I want you to handle this."

"Handle," Wilkes said, "meanin' . . ."

"Kill the Gunsmith," Head said, "kill the journalist, and kill the other man who was here with Adams."

"Who was he?"

"I don't know!" Head said. "Just kill anybody you find with the Gunsmith."

"Okay."

"And try to get it all done," Head said, "without killing my whole political future."

Wilkes got up and lumbered toward the door. "Lumber" was the only way to describe how a man as short and squat as he was could move.

"Um, boss?" he said at the door.

"Yeah?"

"Can I use the Doc's people?"

"You know what?" Head said. "Use whoever you want—and then kill them, too!"

"Gotcha. You, uh, got any idea where they are?"

"No, but if I had to hazard a guess," Head said, "I'd say they were going to go to the asylum and talk to that doctor friend of yours."

"Right," Wilkes said. "That makes sense."

And as Wilkes went out the door, Richard R. Head started thinking about who he could use to kill Wilkes.

***

By the time Jacoby walked in, the place smelled like a restaurant—a top grade restaurant. Nellie had done wonders with what she had.

"Wow, that smells good," Jacoby said.

"You're just in time for supper," Nellie told him.

"That suits me. I'm starvin'."

He washed up and then sat down at the table with Clint. Nellie came with a plate for each of them, then got her own and sat down.

As they started to eat Clint asked, "So how'd you do?"

"I got a doctor who's going to make an appointment for us at the asylum," Jacoby said. "Supposedly, you have a relative who might need to be committed, but you want to see the place first."

"Did you use my real name?"

"No," Jacoby said, "not yours, or mine. As far as they're concerned, one of us is Charles Davis."

"A nice simple name," Nellie said.

"I'm guessin' you'll want to be Davis, and do the talkin'," Jacoby said.

"I think that'll be best, if it's okay with you," Clint responded.

"Hey," Jacoby said, "I'm your back-up. You're the one makin' the play."

"And I'm just supposed to keep hiding here?" Nellie asked.

"Yes!" both Clint and Jacoby said.

"Okay, okay," she said, "just checking."

***

After supper Nellie cleaned up while Clint and Jacoby had a cup of coffee. When she was done she joined them.

"You know," she said, "this reminds me why I wanted a career and didn't want to get married."

"Sorry," Clint said. "Next time I'll clean up."

"Oh, it's all right," she said. "It's not a permanent situation."

"Marriage isn't, either," Jacoby said. Neither Clint nor Nellie asked him if he was speaking from personal experience.

After the coffee Jacoby stood to leave.

"I'll pick you up in the mornin' and we'll go right to Blackwell Island," he said. "I'll arrange for a boat."

"Sounds like a plan," Clint said.

He walked him to the door and made sure it was locked behind him.

"So," Nellie said, as Clint returned to the center of the huge space, "what do we do now?"

"Look for a way to kill time, I guess," he said. "Do you play poker?"

She didn't answer. She was looking at the bed.

Chapter Thirty-Nine

Clint and Nellie spent the night killing time in bed. They did it by agreeing that neither of them would get "too attached."

"This is just us helping each other pass the time," Clint said.

"Right."

So Nellie spent some time sucking on Clint's hard cock until he exploded into her mouth and yelled as loud as he wanted to because no one would be able to hear them . . .

And Clint spent some time down between Nellie's legs, licking and kissing her until she was sopping wet and then thrashing about on the bed uncontrollably and finally screaming because she knew nobody would hear her . . .

And then they spent a lot of the time just kissing . . . each other's mouths, necks, shoulders, chest . . . Clint spending extra time on those little titties of hers . . . her peppering his inner thighs with light kisses . . . before she rolled onto her back and he mounted and entered her . . .

***

In the morning they woke, looked at each other and smiled.

"I'll make breakfast," she said, "and have it ready by the time Jack gets here."

"Yeah," Clint said, "hopefully he wasn't right outside our door at any time."

"Oh God." She covered her mouth. "When did you think of that? I convinced myself there was no way anybody could hear us last night."

"Naw, he probably never came by."

"Let's just hope not."

She stood up, pulled on a robe and walked to the stove.

Clint got out of bed, remained naked until he'd washed himself thoroughly, then got dressed. When he turned he saw that Nellie had been watching him.

"Mind your own business," he said.

She laughed and turned back to her business, which was eggs . . .

***

When Jacoby knocked on the door, both Clint and Nellie were dressed, and she had breakfast ready to put on the table.

"One of us has perfect timing," she said to Jacoby, when he came in.

"I don't care which," Jacoby said, "as long as it smells this good each time I come."

"Have a seat," she said. "It'll be ready in minutes."

Jacoby sat with Clint at the table.

"Did you arrange for a boat?" Clint asked.

"Yes," Jacoby said. "It's at a pier on the East River. We'll have to row to the island."

"How long will that take?"

"Not long."

Nellie covered the table with ham-and-eggs, and they ate.

"I have a question," she announced, halfway through the meal.

"What is it?"

"What if 'Dick' Head has warned the asylum that you're coming?" she asked.

"Anything could happen," Clint said. "Doctor Evander might simply talk to us and lie, or he might set a trap and try to kill us."

"Then why would you go in?" she asked.

"It's the next logical course of action," Jacoby said.

"But you may have to fight," she said. "Just the two of you."

"I've been fighting overwhelming odds all my life," Clint said. "And I always have to feel that with this—" he touched the gun on his hip "—I can come out on top."

"What if you don't?" she asked. "What if you don't come out on top, and you die?"

"That day is coming," he said. "It's inevitable. But I can't be afraid of it."

"I know what you mean," Jacoby said. "We have to live our lives without making decisions based on fear."

"So you agree?" Nellie said. "Both of you. You have to go in there?"

"Yes."

"To save me."

"That's what this is all about," Clint said.

"Well," she said, "Just don't get killed doing it."

That'll be my priority," Clint said, "but it would make a good story for you, wouldn't it?"

"Some things are more important than a story," she responded.

Jacoby frowned. "Are you sure she's a journalist?"

Chapter Forty

Bennett Wilkes entered the office of Dr. Samuel Evander, who frowned.

"This is unusual," he said. "Since the availability of the telephone, that is how we communicate."

"This took the personal touch," Wilkes said.

Evander was in his 60's with grey hair but, somehow, clean, pink-hued skin.

"How's that?"

"You're gonna have a visitor today, Doc."

"Oh? Who?"

"A man named Clint Adams."

"Is that supposed to mean something to me?" he asked.

"That depends," Wilkes said. "How much do you know about dime novels and Western Legends?"

"Not much," the doctor said. "I have more important things to tend to."

"Your patients?"

Doctor Evander lowered his voice. "My new assignments. I have to find the right patients to send out."

"You better hold off for a while," Wilkes suggested.

"Why?"

"I told you," the man said. "You're havin' a visitor."

"This dime novel Western legend you mentioned? Adams?" Evander lowered his eyes to the papers on his desk.

"He's also known as the Gunsmith."

Evander looked up. "Wait. I know that name."

"Yes, you do."

"And he's coming here?"

"Probably today."

"Why?"

"To investigate," Wilkes explained. "He was talking to Assemblyman Head about someone trying to kill a journalist named Nellie Bly."

Evander frowned. "I have no such assignment on my desk."

"No," Wilkes said, "I was taking care of that myself. But she did have intentions of writing about this place. Having her die would have been to your benefit."

"And it still may," Evander said, "but tell me more about this Gunsmith."

"Well," Wilkes said, "here's what I think we should do . . ."

***

Clint and Jacoby arrived at the Woman's Lunatic Asylum after rowing their boat to Blackwell Island.

"My arms are sore," Clint said. "That's not something I've done very much."

"You did a fine job."

When they got to the front gate they gave their names to a guard, who checked his list.

"Go on through," he said.

They walked up to the front entrance, where they were met by a male nurse.

"Follow me, please and don't stray. Some of these patients can be dangerous."

They followed the nurse through halls populated with patients walking back and forth. Some of them had their arms folded, caressing themselves. Others had their hands clenched in their hair. Still others simply stood and rocked.

"They're allowed outside their rooms, like this?" Clint asked.

"It's for exercise," the nurse said. "They'll be back in their rooms, soon."

He led them down several halls until they reached a door with DR. SAMUEL EVANDER written on it. The nurse opened the door and waved them in. He entered behind them.

"These gentlemen are here for an interview, Miss Evans," she told the middle-aged woman sitting at a desk.

"Do they have an appointment?"

"Yes," Clint said. "I'm Charles Davis.

"Ah, yes, Mr. Davis," she said, "the doctor has been expecting you. And this is?"

"My colleague, Mr. Jacoby."

"I'll tell the doctor you're here," she said. "That will be all, nurse."

The nurse nodded, and left.

"I'll be right back," she told them, and went through the door behind them. When she returned she said, "The doctor will see you, now."

"Thank you."

Clint and Jacoby entered the office.

"Mr. Davis?" a 60-ish man asked.

"That's right," Clint said.

"Please, be seated." The man made no attempt to shake hands. Clint and Jacoby took seats, and then the doctor sat down behind his desk.

"I understand you have a relative you believe needs treatment?" the doctor asked.

"Actually," Clint said, "I'm here on another matter, Doctor."

"Really?" the doctor asked. "And what is that?"

"My name is not Charles Davis," he said. "It's Clint Adams. I'm here to talk about murder. Specifically, murder for hire."

"I see. And am I supposed to know what all this means?"

"I believe so," Clint said. "You see, I think you're using your patients to commit murder-for-hire."

"What leads you to that belief?"

"A journalist who was here posing as a patient heard a conversation you had, regarding assassins."

Evander sat back in his chair and made a steeple of his hands.

"I think I know who you mean," he said. "I discovered that we had a journalist here under false pretense, named Nellie Bly. Is this what she was going to write?"

"Actually," Clint said, "Nellie said you knew about her job here and approved it."

"That's preposterous," he said. "I knew no such thing."

"So you never approved her stay?"

"I did not."

"What about the conversation you had, regarding the assassination of a politician named Frank Colton?"

"I believe I know what that was about," Evander said. "We have a patient here who is under the delusion that he's a paid assassin. Perhaps she heard me discussing his treatments?"

"But Frank Colton was assassinated last week!"

"Really?" Evander said, frowning. "Well, that's quite disturbing."

"I believe the police, or even the federal government, might want to come here and talk to you about this."

Evander considered the comment.

"I'll tell you what," he said. "Let me bring that patient in here and you can talk to him. Perhaps we can clear this up."

"Why don't we do that?" Clint agreed.

"I'll only be a minute," Evander said, rising and leaving the room.

"You think they might have such a patient?" Jacoby asked.

"If he's using them as assassins, I think he probably could convince them of anything. Let's wait and see."

A few minutes after the doctor left, the woman from the outer office opened the door.

"The doctor would like you to follow me," she said.

"Of course."

Clint and Jacoby left the office, and approached the door to the hall. She held it open for them, but after they stepped through she closed it behind them, remaining on the other side.

"Ma'am?" Clint said.

Jacoby tried the doorknob. The door was locked.

"We're locked out," he said.

Clint looked down the hall, where several patients were milling about, eyeing them venomously.

"Actually," he said, "I think it's more like we're locked in . . ."

Chapter Forty-One

"This is a trap," Jacoby said.

"Well," Clint said, "we did consider the possibility."

"And we walked in, anyway."

The patients began to come toward them. They noticed that they were all male, and rather large.

"Why don't we see if we can walk out?" Clint asked.

They started down the hall and retraced their steps to the front entrance. When Jacoby tried the doors, he found them locked. The patients were still coming toward them.

"Are they armed?" Clint asked.

Jacoby squinted.

"I think I see some clubs—and is that a knife?"

"Knives and clubs," Clint said.

"No match for our guns."

"But do we want to shoot these men?" Clint asked. "They're innocent pawns of Dr. Evander."

"Pawns or not," Jacoby said, "Look at their eyes. They want to kill us."

Jacoby took out his gun, a short-barreled Colt.

"Wait, wait . . ." Clint said.

"I don't think we can wait," Jacoby said. "If we don't kill them, they'll kill us."

"But how many patients are there in this building," Clint said. "We'll run out of bullets before we run out of patients."

"Well, we have to do something. They're getting closer."

They had their backs to the front doors, pressed right up against them, as the patients got closer and closer.

"Maybe if we fire over their heads they'll run," Clint said.

"And waste bullets?" Jacoby asked. "I'm not waiting any longer."

He pointed his gun at the largest patient he could find, a man in the front. But before he could fire, there was a sound.

The locks on the doors behind them.

Clint turned, tried the doorknob, and found the doors unlocked.

"Come on!" he said, grabbing Jacoby's arm.

They slipped out the doors, and closed and locked them just as the mob reached them. The crazed mob began to beat on the doors, some of them with their faces mashed against the windows.

"Jesus," Jacoby said, holstering his gun.

They were in a foyer. When they tried the outer doors they, too, were unlocked. Outside they found a female nurse waiting for them, a pretty blonde in her 30's.

"Are you Carol Whitney?" Clint asked.

"I am. Who are you?"

"Clint Adams."

"I'm Jacoby."

"You saved us from having to kill a lot of people," Clint said. "Thank you."

"I heard the doctor discussing his plan to have patients kill two men," she said. "But I didn't know who. Are you friends of Nellie Bly?"

"We are," Clint said. "We're trying to help her stay alive long enough to write her story."

"Well, I hope she writes it soon," Nurse Whitney said. "I'm looking forward to getting out of here and finding a job in a real hospital."

"We appreciate what you just did," Clint said, "but did you see where Dr. Evander went?"

"He left in his buggy," she said. "I guess he wanted to be able to say he wasn't here when the patients got free and killed the two of you."

Clint looked back into the hall. It seemed as if a few orderlies, or male nurses, had shown up and were taking the patients away.

"Is there anyone else here like you, who doesn't approve of the practices?" Jacoby asked.

"Maybe a few."

"And are there any who are working with Evander on his sideline?" Clint asked.

Nurse Carol Whitney looked down at her shoes and said, "Maybe a few."

Clint looked at Jacoby.

"We better talk to these people and decide what we're going to do."

***

With the further help of Carol Whitney, they went back inside the building. The patients had all been rounded up and put into their rooms.

"What exactly is your position here?" Clint asked.

"I'm the head nurse. That's why I was able to unlock the front doors for you."

"And what's your opinion of the conditions here?"

"Deplorable!" she said. "I told Nellie that."

"And the fact that patients are being used as assassins?" Jacoby asked. "That's a surprise to you?"

"Very much so," Whitney said. "When Nellie first told me of her suspicions, I didn't believe her."

"And you didn't know anything about it until now?" Clint asked.

"Not a thing," she said. "But with Dr. Evander trying to kill the two of you by using the patients . . ."

"Now you believe it," Jacoby said.

"Oh, yes. And it's horrible!"

They followed Whitney back to Dr. Evander's office, which was now empty. Even his receptionist had gone.

"What about Miss Evans?" Clint asked. "Do you think she was involved?"

"I doubt it," Nurse Whitney said, "but she's devoted to Dr. Evander."

"And who is Evander's second in command?" Clint asked.

"That would be Dr. Weldon."

"Is he here tonight?"

"No, he had the night off."

"Then I guess it's going to fall to you to run this place until other arrangements can be made."

"Oh, God, no," she said. "That's not a job I want."

"Well, as head nurse you have the right to bring people in here to talk to us, don't you?"

"I do."

"Then let's do that," Clint said. "Maybe we can separate the wheat from the chaff."

"The what?" she asked.

"The good from the bad," Jacoby said.

"Oh."

"Come on," Jacoby said, "I'll go with you to get them."

"Uh, which first?" she asked. "The uh, wheat or the, uh . . ."

"Anybody you feel we can count on," Clint said.

"Right."

Chapter Forty-Two

"We're wasting time," Jacoby said to Clint, a couple of hours later.

With Nurse Carol Whitney's help they had a pretty good idea of who they could count on, and who might have been working with the doctor. They had separated a few orderlies, because it made sense that they would be in charge of the patients who were being used as killers.

"What would you rather be doing?" Clint asked.

"We've gotta catch this doctor!"

"How do we do that?" Clint asked. "We don't know where he's gone."

"What about his home?"

"If he's on the run do you think he'd go right there?" Clint asked.

"Well, we have to do something."

"You're right," Clint said.

He looked at the phone on the doctor's desk as Nurse Whitney entered the office.

"Carol, we have to go," he said

"What? What am I supposed to do?"

"Keep the orderlies and nurses you can count on around you. We'll tie the other ones up."

"And then what?"

"Use that phone," Clint said, eyeing the unfamiliar object. "Call the police, and call Dr. Weldon. Get them out here to take care of things. If the police search this office, and all the records, they may find some evidence."

"Where does Evander live?" Jacoby asked.

"He has a house on the island."

That surprised Clint.

"I thought he'd have a place in the city."

"No, he stays here almost all the time."

"Does he have a phone in his house?"

"Yes."

"Goddamnit!" he swore.

"What?" she asked.

"He's thinkin' Evander might have gone there to call whoever his partners are, like Dick Head," Jacoby told her.

"Richard Head, the Assemblyman?" she asked.

"Yes, why?"

"I've heard the doctor talk to Mr. Head's man."

"What man?"

"His name is Wilkes, Bennett Wilkes. In fact, he was here earlier today."

Clint looked at Jacoby. "He must have warned Evander we were coming. It might have even been his idea to set the trap for us to be killed by patients."

"I know Wilkes," Jacoby said. "He'll work for anybody who'll pay him."

"Would he be involved in something like assassination for profit?" Clint asked.

"Oh, yeah."

"Okay," Clint said, "so we have Evander, Wilkes, and Head who are all part of this. And these orderlies here."

"If there's anybody else," Jacoby said, "it's going to be up to the police to find them."

"Right," Clint said, and looked at Whitney. "So we're back to that. Call the police, get them and Dr. Weldon out here as soon as possible."

"What do I tell them?"

"That it's a matter of murder," Clint said. "Tell them you think you know who killed Assemblyman Frank Colton last week. That'll bring them running."

"Do I tell them, about you?"

Clint and Jacoby looked at each other.

"Tell them about me," Jacoby said. "Keep Clint out of it." He looked at Clint again. "This case might keep you here in New York for a long time. I can testify any time."

"Okay, thanks," Clint said.

"What are you going to do?" Nurse Whitney asked.

"Give us an orderly who can take us to Dr. Evander's house," Clint said. "We'll check there first. After that we'll have to go back to town and look for Bennett Wilkes. Maybe we can get him to turn on Assemblyman Head."

Chapter Forty-Three

Whitney gave them an orderly named Stan, who told them that the Doctor's buggy was gone.

"He could have got to the dock on foot and taken a boat, couldn't he?" Clint asked.

"Not the Doc," Stan said. He was in his thirties, a burly man who Whitney said was dedicated to what he did. "He's afraid to leave this island. He never leaves."

"Never?" Clint asked.

"Not for years," Stan said. "I've been here five years, and he's never left."

Clint and Jacoby looked at each other.

"Could we get this lucky?" Clint asked. "That he went right to his house?"

"Let's find out."

"Can we walk there?" Clint asked Stan.

"We could, but there's another buggy and we have a second horse. It'll take me minute to bring it around."

"Do it!" Clint said.

***

They went part of the way on a road, and then Stan pulled over and stopped.

"Now we have to walk from here. It's in the woods."

"How did he find this?" Clint wondered.

"The story goes he was just out walking one day, getting some exercise and, because he never intended to leave this island once he opened the hospital-"

"Hospital?" Clint asked.

"That's what it started out as before he turned it into an asylum," Stan said. "But anyway, he was walkin' and he came upon this rundown house, and had it fixed up for himself."

They started walking off the road while Stan talked, and before long they saw a house in the distance.

"That's it," Stan said, keeping his voice down.

At that moment there was a shot, and a blossom of blood sprouted on Stan's white orderly coat. The man fell over backwards; Clint and Jacoby crouched over him.

"Oh, damn . . ." Stan said.

"Hang on, Stan," Clint said. "Let's take a look."

They moved the coat aside and saw that, while the bullet had hit him in the chest, it had most likely missed his heart. If they got him medical attention fast enough, he'd probably make it.

"We've got to get him back to the buggy," Clint said. "Jack, you'll have to take him back and hope that Dr. Weldon's there."

"What are you gonna do?"

"I'm going to get him out of that house."

"You know he's not alone," Jacoby said, keeping pressure on Stan's wound. "The doctor couldn't have made that shot."

"I know," Clint said, as they picked up Stan and started carrying him back to the buggy. "I'm thinking Wilkes must be in there. He probably stayed on the island to see if the trap worked."

As they reached the buggy and placed Stan into it, the sky opened up and it started to rain. Because it was falling so hard through the tree, and on the ground, they had to shout.

"Get him back there!" Clint said. "He'll make it."

"Be careful!" Jacoby shouted. "I'll get back as soon as I can."

"I can't wait for you!"

"I know!"

Clint slapped the horse on the rump, and Jacoby turned the buggy and headed back to the asylum on the dead run.

Clint turned and ran back through the rain toward the house. He was soaked, and chilled to the skin by the time he got there. In addition to the rain, it had gotten dark, and there was a light in the house, hopefully. The rain and darkness might enable him to get closer, where he could make something happen.

He decided to circle around the back . . .

***

Inside the house Bennett Wilkes was snapping at Dr. Evander, who was sitting in a chair by the fireplace, with a fire going and a snifter of brandy in his hand.

"I told you we should've gotten off this damn island!"

"I'm sorry, but I can't do that, Mr. Wilkes," Evander said. "Why don't you go out the back and make for the dock?"

"Are you kiddin'?" Wilkes said. "That's the goddamned Gunsmith out there." He looked out the window again, a long-barreled Colt in his hand.

"Then I guess you shouldn't have missed him and hit Stan."

"If he comes closer I won't miss him again," Wilkes said, "but I ain't goin' out there to face him." He turned around to look at the doctor. "Why are you so calm?"

"This day had to come," Evander said. "I couldn't operate like this forever. I knew it had to end, and I'm right where I want to be."

"You're crazy!" Wilkes said. "If I knew you were crazy I never would've got involved with you."

"It was the money, and you know it," Evander said sipping his brandy. "That's why I have this good brandy here, even though I haven't left his island in twelve years."

"You been hidin' here all this time, an' don't have a hidin' place in these woods?"

"Yes, I do."

"Well, where is it?" Wilkes said. "We got time to go out the back and get there."

"It's here," Evander said, spreading his hand, "right here."

"Oh damn," Wilkes said, turning around and pointing his gun at Evander. "I should shoot you right now."

Evander took a sip and said, "Do it!"

***

Clint moved through the woods and got around to the rear of the house. There was a back door, and that was all he needed. If Wilkes was inside with a gun, and he was the only one, there was no way he could cover the front and the back.

He broke from cover and started for the rear door, waiting for a shot that never came. When he got to the door he immediately kicked it in, gun in hand.

As he darted through the doorway he saw a man who had to be Bennett Wilkes pointing a gun at the seated Dr. Evander, who seemed unconcerned.

"Don't!" he shouted.

Wilkes turned toward him with his gun, and Clint fired one shot. The gun flew from Wilkes' hand as the bullet spun him, and knocked him to the floor.

Clint turned his gun toward Evander.

"Doctor?"

"Would you like a brandy, Mr. Adams?"

Chapter Forty-Four

When Jacoby got back to the house Clint was waiting with Dr. Evander, and Bennett Wilkes' body.

"It's over?" Jacoby asked, as he came through the front door.

"It's over."

"And the rain has stopped," Jacoby said.

"How's Stan?"

"I don't know," Jacoby said. "I left him with Dr. Windsor, and came back here."

"Windsor's a good man," Evander said. "I'm sorry Stan was shot, but he'll pull him through."

Jacoby looked down.

"So is that Wilkes?" he asked.

"That's him."

"And he works for Richard Head, right?" Clint asked.

"He does."

"And Head's involved with your murder for hire business?" Clint asked.

"He is not," Evander answered.

"What?" Jacoby asked.

"It was just Wilkes and me," Evander said. "But Wilkes did convince Mr. Head to support the asylum."

Clint and Jacoby exchanged a look that said they might not be buying it.

"Well, okay, Doc, let's get back to the asylum and we'll figure all this out."

"I'm afraid I can't do that," Evander said, looking very sleepy.

"Oh? Why's that?" Clint asked.

"There's a reason I came right here after I unleashed the patients on you," the man said. "I knew someone like you would get out, and come after me."

"So you decided to wait here for me to catch you?"

"No," Evander said. "I knew Mr. Wilkes was here, so I figured you'd catch him—or kill him."

"And what did you think I'd do to you?"

"Well," Evander said, "fortunately for you, you're just in time to watch me die." He raised his glass and drained the brandy.

"You mean—" Jacoby said, but he stopped when Evander slumped over, dropping the brandy glass to the floor. It didn't break.

Clint walked over, picked up the glass and sniffed.

"Some kind of poison," he said. "Not hard for a doctor." He straightened and stared down at the man. "Damn it!"

"So they're both dead," Jacoby said. "Now what?"

"There's still Richard Head," Clint said.

"Evander said Head wasn't involved."

"Head's guilty of something," Clint said. "He has to be, with a man like Wilkes working for him. Let's do a search here and see if we can find something—anything that connects them."

Jacoby shrugged. "Okay."

There was a desk in the room, and a chest of drawers. They centered their efforts on them. There were plenty of papers, mostly letters he exchanged with family members, and a book.

Jacoby held it up.

"What is it?" Clint asked.

The detective shrugged.

Clint took it, opened it, skimmed it.

"It's a journal," Clint said. "He seems to have jotted down all his major thoughts here."

"Like why he started a murder for hire business?"

"I'll bet," Clint said, "there's why and how in here, and some other information. We should give it to the police."

"The crooked New York City Police Department?"

"Who else is there?" Clint asked.

Jacoby shrugged again.

"What do we do with them?" he asked, pointing at the two bodies.

"Leave them here," Clint said. "The police can come and pick them up."

"Let them take care of burying them," Jacoby said.

"Right."

***

There were two uniformed policemen at the asylum when they got there. They told them what happened, and the two men said they had called headquarters for a whole crew to be sent out: a detective, a sergeant, and some uniformed men to ask questions and look for evidence.

"To collect evidence," Officer Mead said. "At least, that's what they say their job is."

"Well, there are two dead men in a house not far from here," Clint said. "Arrangements will have to be made to pick them up."

"We'll let the sergeant decide about that," Officer Victor said.

"Fine with me," Clint said. "We have to get back to Manhattan."

"You can't leave the island until the boss gets here," Victor said. "And the detectives. What are your names?"

"My name's Jacoby. His name doesn't matter. He was just along for the ride."

"Still need a name," Mead said.

Clint and Jacoby looked at each other.

"Smith," they said.

Chapter Forty-Five

They didn't want to wait.

Clint knew that eventually his real name would come out. Then he'd be scrutinized, and stuck in New York for a long time. So he and Jacoby agreed to get him the hell off that island.

"There's got to be a back door to this place," Jacoby said. "Find it and get out of here. I'll handle it."

"Okay, thanks."

He found Nurse Carol Whitney in Dr. Evander's office.

"Dr. Windsor says Stan's going to be all right."

"Good," he said to her. "Listen, do you want to get out of here?"

"So bad!" she said.

"Me, too," Clint said. "I can't afford to have the police keep me here indefinitely, so I want to go back to Manhattan now. You show me the back way out of here, and I'll take you with me."

"You've got a deal."

"Do you have something other than your nurse's whites to change into?"

She cocked her hip sexily. "What, you don't like my nurse whites?"

"I love them," he said. "You can change, and bring them with you."

"Deal, and deal," she said. "Follow me."

***

She took him to a back room and changed into her street clothes right in front of him. She had a solid body with nice round breasts and beautiful smooth, pale skin.

"You can look," she told him. "I'm not shy."

"That's good," he said, "because I'm enjoying looking."

"Well," she said, arching an eyebrow at him, "I hope you've got someplace we can go when we get off this island. My address is on file, here."

"Don't worry," he said. "I've got a place."

She stuffed her nurse's whites into a canvas bag, turned to him and said, "Okay, honey. Let's go."

***

Carol Whitney led Clint down several halls until they reached a back door, and then out. The rain had let up and they were able to walk to where he and Jacoby left the rowboat.

Clint rowed all the way back to the dock, where he and Jacoby had left their horse and buggy. He was actually surprised that it was still there.

From there they rode to the safe house building and went upstairs.

"Oh My God, you're finally ba—Carol!"

Nellie ran to Carol and the two women hugged fiercely, and then started chattering.

Nellie had a pot of coffee on the stove, and Clint poured a cup to ward off the chill. He also gave Carol a cup.

"Thank you."

"So?" Nellie asked Clint. "Is it over?"

"Well," he said, "the murder for hire plot out there is done. Dr. Evander is dead, and so is a man named Wilkes, who apparently worked for Assemblyman Head."

"And what about him?"

"He's still around," Clint said, "but the word we got is, he wasn't involved in the murders."

"He didn't try to have me killed?"

"Well, he probably did, but it had nothing to do with the asylum. What were you going to write about him?"

"After I finished my asylum story, I was going to write about why he should never run for Mayor."

"Then I guess he didn't appreciate that. Have you written about him before?"

"A piece here and there," she said, "and nothing flatter-ing."

"Then he may not be done trying to kill you," Clint said. "I'll have to go and see him tomorrow."

"What's happening at the asylum?" Nellie asked. "Where's Jack?"

"The police are there, with Jacoby. Carol and I slipped out the back. She'll need a place to stay until we finish this off."

"Stay here!" Nellie said, clapping her hands.

"Thanks."

"The asylum will either be closed down, or somebody else will be put in charge. After you write your story, my guess is the state will close it down."

"And I'll need a new job," Carol said.

"Any hospital would be lucky to have you!" Nellie announced.

"I agree," Clint said, remembering what Carol looked like in—and out—of her whites.

"So," Clint said, "do we have any food? Jacoby will probably be here late, depending on how long the police keep him, and how mad they are that we ducked out."

"We need some provisions if I'm going to cook for four," Nellie said.

"I'll go and get some," Clint said.

"I'll come with you," Carol said. "I need some things, and I'll help you pick out the food."

"Good," Nellie said. "I'll get started with what we have."

"We'll be back soon," Clint said.

He and Carol went out the door and down the steps, but before he could open that door Carol grabbed his arm, turned him and kissed him fervently. He returned the kiss with equal vigor.

"Are you and Nellie involved?" she asked, breathlessly.

"No," he said.

"Good, but we won't be able to do anything upstairs, so . . ."

She fell down to her knees, unbuttoned his trousers, and fished out his semi-hard cock.

"Jesus, Carol—" he said, but he didn't fight her.

She stroked him until he was good and hard and then took him into her hot mouth. He was excited, she was proficient at what she was doing, and it wasn't long before he was shooting into her mouth.

"There," she said, standing and wiping the corners of her mouth with her fingers, "that should hold you."

"And what's going to hold you?" he asked.

"Oh, I can wait—"

"I don't think so."

He pushed her down on the stairs, grabbed her pants and pulled them off. Luckily, they were loose fitting. He got down on his knees, pressed his face to her fragrant, golden pubic patch and ate her pussy until she was gushing all over his face.

"There," he said, standing, and wiping his face on his sleeve, "that should hold you."

"Omigod!" she gasped, getting her breath back. "It better!"

Chapter Forty-Six

They waited to eat until Jacoby showed up, even though it was late.

"They were gonna hold me for lettin' you slip out," he said to Clint.

"What happened?" Carol asked.

"I managed to talk them out of it."

"How?" Nellie asked.

"By lettin' the detectives take the credit for closin' down a murder for hire business at the asylum."

The police didn't need Clint, and didn't want Jacoby. They were taking all the credit.

Over a sumptuous meal prepared by Nellie—with Carol's help—they discussed their options.

"There's only one," Clint said, swallowing a piece of perfectly cooked beef. "We've got to go and see Head and convince him to leave Nellie alone, and not to run for Mayor."

"That's all?" Jacoby asked.

"That's it."

"Carol and I will stay here and wait," Nellie said. "At least now I'll have some company."

"We'll go and do that in the morning," Clint said. "Nellie, who did it look like Head was going to run against?"

"Well, there's the incumbent, who's running for reelection," she said.

"Okay," Clint said. "And?"

"One other man," she said. "Although he hasn't said for sure he's going to run, but rumors say that he is."

"And who's that?"

"Herman MacDonald."

***

Clint and Jacoby went to see MacDonald the next morning.

"What can I do for you fine gentlemen?" the teamster leader asked, sitting back in his desk chair.

"You can tell us if you intend to run for Mayor," Clint said.

"Well," MacDonald said, "I have been thinkin' about it, but I'd have to run against the incumbent, and against Richard Head."

"Maybe not," Clint said.

"That's an interestin' comment," MacDonald said. "Tell me more."

***

Jacoby got them into Head's building, and Herman MacDonald got them into his office.

"I'm sorry, Mr. Head," the Assemblyman's girl said, "they just burst in past me."

Head looked up at Clint, Jacoby, MacDonald and several of his teamsters.

"That's okay," he said. "You can go."

201

She backed out of the room and closed the door.

"Dick," MacDonald said. "Dickie. How're you doin'?"

"What's this all about, Herman?" Head asked. "Why are you here, with them?"

"Well, they came to see me this mornin' and told me a very interestin' story. It's about murder for hire and your man, Wilkes."

"Hey," Head said, pointing at MacDonald, "that was all Wilkes and that crazy doctor out there."

"Out where?" MacDonald asked.

"The asylum."

"Oh, so you did know all about it?"

"I, uh, well, I didn't, but then—"

"You know, Dickie," MacDonald said, "I think I just decided to run for Mayor. And do you know why?"

"Why?"

MacDonald smiled. "Because you won't be. That is, unless you want it to get out that you were involved with a murder for hire ring."

"But I wasn't!"

"Yeah," MacDonald said, "but the word will get out, anyway." He looked at Clint and Jacoby. "You fellas can go. We got this."

"There's one more thing," Clint said.

"Oh yeah," MacDonald said, turning his attention back to Head. "That journalist, Nellie Bly? If anythin' happens to her, then the word will definitely get out. And you'll be done in politics for good. Got it?"

Head swallowed. "I got it."

"We good?" MacDonald asked Clint.

"We're good, Herman. Th-thanks."

"Don't mention it, Clint," MacDonald said.

Clint and Jacoby left the room. Head's girl looked up from her desk with frightened eyes.

"It's okay, sweetie," Clint said. "Nothing's going to happen to your boss."

"But," Jacoby said, "you might want to start lookin' for a new job.

Chapter Forty-Seven

Clint ran his hand down Carol Whitney's naked spine until he reached her butt, then ran his palms over each globe. She stirred, turned her head and looked at him.

"I like that you sleep on your stomach," he said.

"Sometimes," she told him, "I sleep on my back."

"Don't get me wrong," he said. "I like that, too."

Once Nellie Bly left the safe house and went home to resume her life again, Clint decided to stay there rather than move to a hotel. Carol decided to stay there with him. It had now been two days, and was the morning Clint would be leaving New York.

"Are you ready to go, already?" she asked. "It's so early."

"No," he said, "not ready to go to the train station." He leaned over and kissed her back. "Just ready to go."

She rolled over, showing him her heavy, pink-tipped breasts and that golden patch, in all their glory and said, "I thought you'd never ask."

***

Nellie, Carol and Jacoby all accompanied him to the train station.

"I don't know how to thank you," Nellie Bly said, hugging him. "You saved my life. I mean, literally. I'm alive and have my life back, all because of you."

"Don't forget they helped," he said, indicating Carol and Jacoby.

"Oh, I won't!' she said. "Believe me."

She backed away so Carol could hug him.

"Thank you," he said to her.

"My pleasure," she said, then whispered in his ear, "believe me."

Nellie and Carol walked away, leaving Clint there with Jacoby.

"How's Delvecchio?" Clint asked.

"Gettin' out tomorrow. He told me you stopped in to see him." the detective told him. "Too bad you can't wait another day, we could do the town."

"Oh, no," Clint said, "I'm ready to go now. Like Nellie said, I've got to get back to my life." He put his hand out and Jacoby shook it. "Thanks for all your help."

"No problem," Jacoby said. "If you're ever this way again, look me up."

"If I ever need a private detective in New York again," Clint assured him, "it'll be a tough choice between you and Del."

"I'll tell him you said so."

The train started to move, so Clint got on it. He turned to wave, but Jacoby was gone.

Coming Soon!

THE GUNSMITH
431
The Science of Death

Now Available

**Lady Gunsmith 1
A New Adult Western Series**

Roxanne Louise Doyle is Lady Gunsmith,
a hot, sexy woman who is unmatched with a gun…

By
AWARD-WINNING AUTHOR
J.R. Roberts

**For more information
visit:** www.speakingvolumes.us

Coming Spring 2018

Lady Gunsmith 5
The Portrait of Gavin Doyle

For more information
visit: www.speakingvolumes.us

Now Available

ANGEL EYES *series*
by
Award-Winning Author
Robert J. Randisi (J.R. Roberts)

Visit us at